I SAW MOMMY KISSING THE NANNY

SHANNON O'CONNOR

Cover by Alt19 Designs

Edited by Beth Hale of Magnolia Author Services

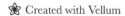 Created with Vellum

I SAW MOMMY Kissing THE Nanny

SHANNON O'CONNOR

I SAW MOMMY
Kissing THE Nanny
Playlist

Shh...Don't Say it - FLETCHER

Mistletoe - Justin Bieber

Her Body is Bible - FLETCHER

Santa Tell Me - Ariana Grande

Like it's Christmas - Jonas Brothers

Bring Me Love - John Legend

All I Want for Christmas is You - Mariah Carey

Santa Baby - Ariana Grande & Liz Gillies

My Only Wish (This Year) - Britney Spears

Have Yourself a Merry Little Christmas - Sam Smith

Underneath the Tree - Kelly Clarkson

Love of My Life - Harry Styles

I'd Be Your Wife - Mary Lambert

ONE

Morgan

"I quit!" I throw my apron on the bar and storm out the front door without hesitation.

The air is chillier than I expected. Part of me wishes I thought to grab my jacket on the way out but there was no way I was going back in right now. I made my choice and I need to live with it. Sure it was impulsive, but I can't work there anymore. I take out my phone and call my friends, hopefully they are still in the city tonight.

"Are you sure you don't want to talk about it?" Bella asks, sipping her mojito slowly. I'm on my second round of shots with Ellie, but Bella is sticking to her two drink maximum to keep a clear head.

Ellie and I look at each other and then say in unison, "No."

Ellie is going through her own breakup with her on and off again girlfriend. They are once again off and Ellie is drinking to get over it. We have a system, numb the inside pain with alcohol and ignore the feelings. It doesn't work great, but it is our system. I have just quit the only job I had and desperately need to pay for college next semester. I have already lost out on being in school this semester due to a lack of funds.

"You could always come work with me," Bella reminds me. I nod but don't say anything. It's not like I am judging her, being an escort is legit work. But it definitely isn't meant for me.

"What about that nanny job you told me about?" Ellie perks up.

"What nanny job?" I look at Bella confused.

"Oh, one of the women I've been out with mentioned her friend needing a nanny. She thought maybe I'd know someone who was interested," she says with a shrug, her jet black hair lightly bouncing.

"You didn't think of me?" I am literally going to college to become a teacher, I already have half degree in education.

"You were working at the bar, I didn't know you'd quit," she says with a chuckle.

"Well, call your work friend. Get me an interview!" I say, picking up her phone and handing it to her.

"Are you sure? I think it's a live in nanny position."

"I'm desperate. I can't get a teaching job until I finish my degree, and I can't finish my degree until I can meet minimum payments again." I sigh. Fuck the government for telling me my *parents* make too much money when I am the one paying for my own college.

"Okay, but let me text her." She smiles. Her fingers dance across the keys with a small smile on her face.

"You'd really live at someone's house and nanny their kid?" Ellie asks, raising an eyebrow.

"I mean that's no rent payment on top of being paid to basically babysit. I don't see the big deal." I shrug. I've had worse jobs.

"She said she's going to text her friend and see when

she can get you an interview," Bella announces with a smile.

"Thank you!" I hug my friend tightly and down another shot. "Now to make this night even better, let's find someone to go home with."

"Oh no, not me," Bella says shyly. One night stands aren't her cup of tea, which confused Ellie and I when she told us her idea to be an escort. She said she only had to go on dates with guys and at least she was being paid if it was a crappy time.

"I already see my type." Ellie pushes her large breasts together, pulling her shirt down just enough to expose them, and fluffs her bright pink hair. "See you guys."

She makes her way across the bar to the blonde with pixie cut short hair and begins chatting her up immediately. It is no secret she has a type, but it is always impressive how quickly she can put the moves on and get someone to buy her a drink or take her home.

"What about you?" Bella asks.

She knows my type is a little more particular. I'm not much of a relationship gal, so I tend to go for the one night stand type. Which varies depending on the day of the week and the crowd of the bar. Tonight I haven't noticed anyone yet but the night is still young. Trying to flag down our bartender with no luck, I decide to go to the actual bar and get them myself. My buzz is starting to wear off and that just won't do.

"Good luck, he's been flirting with that blonde at the end of the bar for twenty minutes," a woman says as I try to get the attention of the only bartender.

I'm about to make a sassy comment when I notice the woman for the first time. She's got this beautiful blonde hair cascading down her back, and despite being at least a good decade older than me, she is exactly my type. I straighten up a little and smile at her.

"Can I buy you a drink?"

"If you can get his attention, sure." She laughs lightly.

"Yo! I need a drink please!" I shout toward the bartender. He looks annoyed but walks over.

"Yes?"

"A vodka cranberry and whatever she's having," I pull out my wallet.

"I'll have the same," the woman says with a smile. The bartender gets us both, then goes on to help the other customers he had been ignoring.

"I'm impressed, I thought I'd be going home sober at that rate," the woman jokes.

"Well, we can't have that, can we?" I tease. "I'm Morgan."

"Lucy." She shakes my hand.

"Do you come here often?"

"Oh my gosh, please don't tell me that's your line. That was absolutely terrible." She laughs.

"No, I actually mean it. I come here a lot with friends and I've never seen you before."

"Maybe you just didn't notice me." She shrugs.

"Oh no, I would've noticed *you*."

A blush creeps across her cheeks and I smile. There is an ease about her I haven't felt with other women. Something that makes me want to get to know her, learn more about her, not just her body. Of course that doesn't stop me when the words slip from her lips.

"Do you want to get out of here?"

TWO

Lucy

The blonde bartender shoots me a look but doesn't say anything when I down the double of whiskey and ask for a second. It was just that kind of a day. Work had been meeting after meeting, while I got into a fight with my son's father *again*. I thought the fighting would end when we got divorced but apparently you can't be so lucky when you have to coparent a child with them. To top things off, my nanny is going on early maternity leave and I'll be without a nanny earlier than expected. Right smack in the beginning of the school year when all the good nannies are committed for the year. My assistant, Kayla, is on it but who knows who she can find on such short notice.

The bar is filled with more college age women than my age but I wasn't in the mood to run into anyone I knew. Noel is sleeping over at a friends house tonight and I am in search of something to take my mind off life. Which is why I'm bolder than usual when the brunette with the dazzling golden eyes and ass that is tighter than my prenup. I'm not typically the '*take a woman home for the night*' kind but I am tired of sticking to what I am supposed to do. She is in this bar, so I know she is at least of age, plus she is funny and beautiful. *What more do I need in a one night stand?*

"Your place or mine?" Morgan asked.

"Yours." I finish my vodka cranberry and hop off the barstool. I'm a little light on my feet so she steadies me. I'm not drunk, just clumsy.

"Let's go." She leads the way to a cab outside. She rattles off her address that isn't too far from here and I feel her playing with the hem of my skirt.

"So overdressed for a college bar," Morgan murmurs in my ear. She keeps an eye on the cab driver as she slides a hand up my thigh, following the slit in my skirt and getting dangerously close to my core.

"We're here." She smirks when the cab stops and I have to collect myself. She pays the driver and holds out a hand, I take it desperate for more of her touch.

Morgan pulls me into her, brushing my hair out of my eyes and holds my chin for a brief second. The eye contact is intense and sends a shock down my spine. Her lips get dangerously close to mine and I close the distance, wanting to know what she tastes like. Soft, pillowy lip-gloss-covered lips meet mine and we are a tangle of tongues on the sidewalk. Neither of us caring who might be looking or what time it is. Our bodies desperate for the touch of each other, she finally pulls apart to lead me upstairs into her apartment.

She pulls me into one of those old elevators where you have to pull the gate closed. Then she pushes me against the wall, and her lips find my neck, gently kissing and nibbling.

"I want you," she murmurs against my skin. Her warm breath raising goosebumps.

The elevator stops and she pulls the gate open, leading me into her apartment. She tears off her jacket and it finds a place on the kitchen table as she takes my hand, I follow her to her room. The second the door shuts, her body is against mine. Her leg finds a spot between my legs, her hands on my hips as she begins to undress me. She unbuttons my shirt with achingly sexy eye contact. Each button going slower than the last until I rip off my blouse and throw it to the ground in sexual frustration. I unzip my pencil skirt and let it fall to my feet. Morgan smirks as she takes in my body. I'm only a little self conscious feeling so on display. So I tug at her jeans and she kicks them to the corner.

"I want to taste you," she murmurs against my lips.

"Fuck, please." I nod. It has been too long since someone had gone down on me. The thought of my ex husband and how he thought it was a chore fires through my head. I push the thought of him out just as quickly when Morgan drops to her knees.

I can feel her breath on my thighs, she tugs down my thong with her teeth and my core is on fire. She stops to reach for my breasts, covered by a thin flimsy bralette. My nipples are two tiny pebbles begging to be touched. Morgan ducks between my thighs and licks carefully. Her tongue lapping up all of my wetness as she keeps eye contact with me. I can feel myself getting even wetter.

"Oh!" A moan leaves my lips as she slips two fingers inside me. Her tongue working over my clit as her fingers start to work me from the inside. She picks up the pace, working both as fast as she can, and I can't help but throw my head back in pleasure.

"Don't stop!" I beg, grasping her thick, dark hair as she continues to eat pussy like there's no tomorrow. I'm on the brink of an orgasm and she continues the pace, flicking her tongue over my clit in the perfect way to make me scream.

"I'm cumming!" I call out but she doesn't stop, her

tongue writing me a love letter as her fingers dance inside me. As my legs shake, she stops to wipe her face on my inner thighs and kisses my core one last time.

We both fall back into her bed, as she climbs on top of me and I wait for her touch. Throwing my head back into her pillows that smell like her, a mix of peppermint and something fresh. Morgan throws off her t-shirt and looks for something in her closet. I'm in too much of a orgasm haze to ask what she's looking for. I can't recall the last time someone besides myself gave me an orgasm. Then Morgan stands at the end of the bed and I'm immediately soaked at the sight of her. She was wearing a hot pink strap on and nothing else.

"Can I fuck you?" she whispers with a small smirk.

"Yes, please." I nod.

She carefully climbs on top of me, spreading her thighs so she's perfectly between my legs. Morgan begins to kiss me, our lips begging for each others. She stops to bite my bottom lip, something I didn't know I'd enjoy. It's when she moans into my mouth that I'm a goner. There is something inherently sexy about that. Her thin fingers find their way from my shoulders down my waist and to my core. She slides one finger up and down my slit, soaking up my wetness and rubs it on her strap. Taking the time to make sure it's soaked, she gives me a final look as if to double check and I nod, biting my bottom lip. The second she slips inside me, I'm moaning harder than before.

"Holy shit," I groan and she slides my leg over her shoulder, hitting in just the perfect spot. Both our breaths are shallow as she bucks her hips to fuck me.

Slipping a finger between my legs, I rub small circles on my clit as she leans down to kiss me. Her soft skin and pillowy lips becoming too much for me. Her lips crushing mine as we battle for dominance although it's clear who has it.

"I want you to cum for me," she says against my lips and my eyes flutter open. Watching her kiss me and feeling her slip in and out of me sends me over the edge. I tremble, moaning as she hits my g-spot perfectly to make me cum.

"God, you're so hot when you cum." Morgan smirks and kisses me softly. I throw my head back on the pillows and smile. After a minute, Morgan takes off her strap and lays next to me. She lets me catch my breath and then I'm climbing between her legs to return the favor.

"You don't have to," she whispers.

"I want to," I say, eyes full of lust. I am dying to know what she tastes like and the sounds she makes when she comes.

Morgan is already soaked, fully ready to be fucked when my tongue meets her pussy for the first time. She tastes as sweet as she looks, so I lap it up. Sucking gently on her clit and licking up and down her slit. Twisting my tongue around to tease her a bit.

"Give me more," she begs, pushing my head down lightly.

I laugh against her, teasing her. I know what she wants but I am having too much fun letting her beg for it. My nails are longer than they probably should be for this so I'm careful, sliding in slowly and curling them gently. Morgan begs for more and I begin to see what a glutton for punishment she is.

"How bad to you want it?" I ask curling a finger inside her, our eyes meeting.

"So fucking bad." She whimpers.

"Tell me how bad." I smirk.

"If you don't fuck me, in a second I'll start doing it

myself." She meets my eyes and I consider my options. As much as it would be hot to watch that, I start to pump my fingers, watching as she gasps out in pleasure. Diving back into her pussy, I give her everything as I devour her.

"Right there!" she calls out after a while and bucks her hips to my face. I keep the tempo and watch as the orgasm builds, she clenches her jaw and a smile spreads across my face as I get an idea.

"Call out my name," I whisper "Or I stop." She nods furiously and I smile. Swirling my tongue across her clit, I watch as she throws her head back in pleasure.

"Oh, Lucy!" She bellows and I smile against her core.

"That was lovely." I wipe my mouth on the back of my arm and climb into bed with her.

"That was hot." She kisses my lips and moans at the taste.

"Don't you start again." I laugh.

"Do you want to spend the night? It's kind of late to grab a cab," Morgan asks as she throws a sheet over us.

"Sure." I nod. I send a quick text to the nanny, letting her know I'll be home in the morning before work. It is rare I stay out all night and it is already three am, it's not like they are waiting around for me.

There's a few work texts that I ignore, but I answer Kayla back about the new interviewee. She has time in the morning to meet with her and if all goes well, I can meet with her before work. I send back an approval and turn into Morgan's arms. Both of us falling asleep quickly in our post orgasm haze, desperate to get some sleep before the morning.

THREE

Morgan

My roommate, Tyra, knocks on my door and I hop out of bed, grabbing the sheet to cover myself. "Yes?" I ask confused.

"Your phone keeps going off, it was in the kitchen in your jacket," she explains, handing me my phone with a yawn. Glancing at the time, it is barely past six am. It rings again when she closes the door but I step into the bathroom to answer it, careful not to wake Lucy.

"What's going on?"

"Dude, why didn't you pick up?" Bella asks from the other end.

"I was sleeping, what's going on?" I ask with a yawn.

"I got you an interview as the live in nanny. But they want to meet you today, at seven."

"In the morning?" My eyes widen as I glance at myself in the mirror. I look like a hot mess, no way I can go to an interview like this.

"Yes, you need to get your butt there. They're making decisions today," she explains.

"Fuck. Well, thank you, but I better go," I say, scrambling.

"Good luck!" she says before hanging up.

I rush back into my bedroom where Lucy is still fast asleep. I'm torn, do I just wake her up and tell her to go or do I let her sleep? I am pretty sure this was a one time thing, although after what she did with her tongue last night I definitely wouldn't mind seeing her again. I throw the sheet over her bare body and search my closet for something professional to wear. I settle on a sweater than can hide most of my tattoos, paired with an overall dress and some tights. I know people are still pretty judgement when they came to tattoos, which sucks but I'm not trying to mess up my chances. I desperately need this job. I decide not to wake Lucy up and duck out with just a note. It's lame but we both knew what it was going into it. I race to the train and manage to make it to the doorstep by six fifty-nine am.I ring the doorbell and wait for someone to answer. The place is nice, a large brownstone with its own entrance. Someone answers the door shortly with a firm smile.

"You must be Morgan, I'm Kayla," the thin, older looking woman says. Her hair is greying and she has a pair of oversized glasses on.

"Pleasure to meet you." I smile and shake her hand.

"Miss Mars is out at the moment but she should be home soon, why don't we start the interview in the study?" she asks, but it's more of a statement. I nod and follow behind, trying not to gawk at how beautiful the inside of the house was. The extra high ceilings, the beautiful art on the walls and the furniture all pull the place together. It looks like a sophisticated house while also looking lived in. Which is something you didn't see often on the Upper East Side.

"So, what made you want to apply for a live in nanny position?" Kayla asks as we both take a seat at the desk.

"I was looking for a new job as my last wasn't the best fit, and my friend Bella told me about the opportunity. I'm going to school for education to be a teacher so I thought this would be a good fit for me to figure out what grade level I might want to work with."

"And where do you currently go to school?"

"I'm enrolled at Eternal Port Valley University, but I took this semester off to be able to pay for next semester," I say shyly.

"Miss Mars has friends who work on the faculty there," she muses.

"What does Miss Mars do?" I realize I forgot to ask Bella last night.

"She works in publishing, I'm not sure if you've heard of the Mars imprint?"

"She runs the Mars imprint? They're one of the biggest publishers in New York," I say in awe.

"Are you a big reader?" she asks, impressed.

"Yes. I mean I read a lot for school but I also like to read in my spare time."

"That might come in handy if you get the job." She smiles and writes something down.

"Now let's go over some expectations of the job and see if you have any questions," Kayla says and I nod.

"Okay, so you'd be responsible for Noel to bring him to school in the morning by seven thirty sharp, pick him up after school and bring him to any extracurricular activities he has or bring him home. Miss Mars doesn't get home until around seven pm and she prefers to put him to bed but you'd be responsible for dinners and making sure the house is in order. Just some light tidying and keeping things up to standard." I nod so she continues. "You'd be asked to live here to make things easier on Miss Mars as sometimes she has a last minute meeting or commitment or overnight plans."

"That's perfectly fine."

"With that said, you'd be allowed to do your own thing during the day and at night once Miss Mars relieves you. She doesn't expect you to be held prisoner here or anything," she says with a laugh. I smile, starting to relax. It would be a lot of commitment but it didn't seem like anything crazy being asked of me.

"Do you have any questions for me?"

"I guess the pay and what my living arrangements would look like?"

"This is the pay." She passes me a post it with a number written on it, and I have to keep my jaw from dropping. It is enough to pay for next semester and more.

"Why don't you come meet Noel and we can finish the second part of the interview there?" she suggests. I follow her through the house toward a living room where a small blonde boy is watching tv and eating cereal.

"Noel, this is Morgan. She might be your new nanny." Kayla smiles.

"Hi, Noel," I wave instead of shaking his hand. It just feels weird shaking a kid's hand after all.

"Hey." He smiles and turns back to his show. Thankfully it's something I recognize.

"Which episode of *Bluey* is this?"

"You know *Bluey*?" He turns around surprised.

"Of course! I love her." I smile. Thankful for the many TikToks I've seen about the blue dog show.

"This is my favorite episode, 'keepy uppy'. Do you want to watch it with me?"

I look to Kayla and she nods so I take a seat on the couch near him. Not too close but not too far away either.

We both watch as he slurps up his cereal and I relax a tiny bit. When the seven minute episode is over, I stand and wait for Kayla to give me more instructions.

"I think Miss Mars would find you as a good fit. Considering I've been her assistant for over a decade, I can say that pretty clearly. Let me show you the room and by then Miss Mars should be here to meet you." She smiles.

"Okay." That was surprisingly easier than I expected.

She leads me down the hallway past four other closed doors. She points out Noel's room and then stops at the last door to show me my room. It has an oversized queen bed, a wall of closet space, a desk and a flat screen tv. It looks more like a hotel room than a guest room, but to each his own. I definitely wouldn't mind living here for the next eight weeks.

"So, what do you think?" Kayla prompts.

"I can definitely make this work." I say with a smile.

"Perfect." She checks her watch. "Let me check on Miss Mars and then we can—"

"Kayla! Kayla! I'm here!" A voice calls down the hallway.

"Excuse me." Kayla walks out of the room leaving me to gawk by myself. It doesn't have any windows but is somehow still beautifully bright with the all white furniture. I could see myself reading books or studying in here.

"Sorry I'm late. I had an early client meeting, but I'm Miss Mars. It's a pleasure to meet you." When I turn around to shake my new boss's hand, my jaw drops. Standing before me is the woman who cried out my name after I gave her leg shaking orgasms last night. Lucy is my new boss? And just like that, I watch the prospect of my dream job vanish into thin air. All because I had to sleep with the boss.

FOUR

Lucy

As the brunette woman turns around, I feel my jaw drop. No way was the woman before me the same woman who made me cum multiple times last night. Her entire demeanor is different. I mean it makes sense, last night she was picking up a woman and today she is applying to be a nanny. Which makes sense why she ran out of her own apartment so quickly last night. Part of me had wondered if she didn't have as much fun as I had.

"Miss Mars, Lucy, nice to meet you." She shakes my hand like it's the first time we're meeting and I'm eternally grateful. I don't hide the fact that I am bisexual, but I don't need my assistant knowing I was out getting laid last night either.

"Kayla, can you grab me a copy of Noel's schedule for the month while I talk to Miss White?" I smile at my assistant and she nods. I wait a moment before closing the door behind her.

"What are you doing here?" I ask panickedly.

"Applying for a job," she says nervously. "I didn't know you were married."

"What? No, his father and I are divorced."

"Oh, thank god." She lets out a long breath. "So I guess my chance just flew out the window, right?"

"Do you really want this job?" I ask, giving her a hard look.

"I do. I know our past might make it complicated, but it's truly a coincidence I'm here. And that's the only reason I left this morning," she adds.

"Do you think you can put last night in the past?" I ask, looking over the papers Kayla gave me. She is the most qualified candidate we've had all week. Kayla told me she thought this was the one and to get her approval isn't easy.

"Of course." She nods and I hesitate.

"If we can both be professional, I don't see why this can't work out." I force a smile just in time for Kayla to come back.

"Here you go." She hands me the schedule and I glance at it. I know most of it by heart, but I have to make this look convincing.

"I'd like to officially offer you the job. Frankly you're the most qualified candidate we had so if you can, I'd love for you to start today."

"Like move in today?"

"You can take time to figure out living arrangements but try to move in here by the end of the month?" I look at my watch, it was already the fifteenth. I don't know how long she'll need to move her stuff her or what her leasing situation is.

"That works." She nods.

"Great, Kayla can you get her all the necessary paperwork? I'll take Noel to school on the way to work."

"Of course." Kayla ushers Morgan out of the room and I let my shoulders relax. This is the right thing to do, right? I mean it shouldn't matter that I had a one night stand with her. She is the most qualified for the job. Plus last night she was incredibly kind and affectionate, all the things you'd want in a lover *and a nanny*.

"Ready to go, Mama?" Noel asks, standing before me with his backpack and jacket on.

"Give me five minutes, kiddo." I smile and rush to my room. I am still wearing the same outfit as last night and I desperately need to change. I wipe my armpits, spray some strategically placed perfume, and change into a work appropriate outfit.

"All set." I smile to Noel as I throw on a jacket and my work heels.

"How come you didn't come home last night?" Noel asks as we walk to school. It was only a few blocks away and I like the extra time with him.

"I had a work meeting that ran late downtown," I lie. But what am I supposed to do, say I was having sex with your new nanny? I blush at the thought. Hopefully I'll be able to move past this, for Noel's sake.

"Oh, do you have another meeting tonight?" He looks at me expectantly with his father's smile and my blue eyes.

"Nope, tonight I'm all yours. We can have a movie night if you'd like. I should be home after dinner." My phone buzzes in my pocket but I ignore it. On my time with Noel, no one else is important. They can wait.

"Okay! What can we watch? Something scary? Something funny? A grown up movie? Dad let's me watch those but I wasn't supposed to tell you that. Whoops. Don't tell Dad." He covers his mouth.

"Oh yeah? What else goes on at Dad's house?" I ask, raising an eyebrow.

"He lets me stay up late and play those video games you don't like," he admits.

"I see." I try to keep a straight face but I'm sure he

already knows I'll be calling his father later. Although it seems like a waste of my breath. Noel's father is one of the most infuriating men I've ever met, how we ended up married is still beyond me. We had a good few years of marriage and then it all went downhill with his immaturity and our arguing. We've been divorced for three years now but it should've been longer.

"Mom?" Noel prompts and pulls me out of my rage spiral.

"Sorry, sweetie, what?"

"Oh, I asked if Tyler could come over to play this week?"

"I'm sure that's okay. I'll call his mom and set something up." I smile.

"Awesome! We can play that new game you got me." He throws his fist in the air and cheers.

"Sounds good, maybe he can teach us how to beat level five," I joke.

"Oh yeah, he's already on level ten, I'm sure he could." Noel shakes his head, more excited.

"Have a great day, sweetie." I give him a quick kiss on his head and he hugs my legs before anyone at school sees. Because apparently it's uncool to hug your mother goodbye.

"Bye, Mama!" he calls and runs into the building. I wait until his teacher waves back, knowing that she got him before I hail a cab to work. I have enough time to get there on time if I grab a cab right now instead of relying on the unreliability of the subway systems.

My work best friend, Dylan, is waiting for me in my office with a large black iced coffee. "I'd kiss you right now," I praise her, thankful for the caffeine. *How had I left the house without some?*

"I think you did enough of that from what I've heard." She smirks, her light pink lips.

"What do you know?" I raise an eyebrow as I take a seat at my desk.

"That your one night stand is your new nanny." She waits for me to confirm it.

"How do you even know that already?" I glare.

"Your new nanny is best friends with Bella." She pauses. We both have an unspoken agreement not to ask about the nature of her relationship with Bella. The less I know, the better.

"I see, so you're about to have a look into my private life?"

"Oh please, like she'd risk her job. That's all I know from Bella and I had to pull that out of her. I wanted all the details from you." She winks.

"There's no details. It was a one time thing, turns out she's the most qualified for the job so I hired her. There's not going to be any weirdness because it's not weird." I shrug.

"Hmm, I thought there would be more than that." She purses her lips. Dylan fluffs her dark hair over her shoulder and takes a sip of her light iced coffee.

"I'm a simple woman. Now get out of here so I can get some work done."

"I'm going, I'm going." She laughs.

My work assistant, Becca, left a bunch of notes on my desk about phone calls to return and agreements to read over. I sigh before logging in to check my email and make sure I'm not missing any meetings right now. I get a text from Morgan and I ignore the way my heart beats a little bit faster as I open it in anticipation.

Morgan: *Moved some of my stuff into the apartment today, can't get out of my lease until next month so technically I have two homes until the 1ˢᵗ. Hope that's okay.*

Me: *Sounds good, thank you.*

It takes me almost ten tries of writing and re-writing to finally text her back. I don't know what I am so nervous about, but I know I will miss those leg shaking orgasms she had given me. I just need to put it in a box and lock it away. It's not like I can be one of those people having an affair with the nanny.

FIVE

Morgan

Leaving my apartment behind is going to be easier than I thought. My roommate, Tyra, and I had moved in together not because we were close friends or even because we had a lot in common, but because we both needed help paying for a two bedroom in the city. But the last few months she's been hinting about her boyfriend moving in and honestly, that guy is the worst of the trash she's dated. So as much as I like having my own place, it will be nice to not have to see her ex boyfriend smoking a bong half naked in the living room while I am trying to get ready for work. I paid until next month and then she would add her boyfriend to the lease and take off my name, she was surprisingly easy going about it.

I pack up my essentials into some boxes I grabbed on the way home and label them myself. Mostly just clothes, soaps, and bathroom essentials and shoes. Along with some of the books I am currently reading. I like having something to do on the subway on my way to work, which of course doesn't apply anymore but I am sure I'll have some downtime to read. Like when Noel is at school or at one of his many classes his mom enrolled him in. When I got a copy of his schedule, I almost fell on the floor. This kid is more well rounded than half the adults I know. Speaking of which, I check the clock on my nightstand and realized if I am going to get these boxes to the apartment in time to pick up Noel from school, I need to leave now.

With my new working bonus, I decide to call a cab to help me haul my stuff instead of trying to lug it on the subway. It is only a lift uptown and with the traveling stipend that I am allowed, I can afford it. So I lug my boxes into the elevator, downstairs into a cab, and I'm on my way to starting my new life as a live in nanny...with the woman I slept with last night.

Noel's school is a simple walk from their apartment, so after grabbing the keys from Kayla, I'm on my way to get him. I'm early, but I am worried about being late and getting lost on my first day. I mean why do elementary schools have so many freaking exits and entrances. Noel is in the second grade so I find the door marked so and wait with all the other nannies and parents. Fifteen minutes later, a parade of screaming children come running out. The teachers attempting to wrangle them, but clearly losing that battle. Noel is one of the quieter ones, he's talking to another boy but he's not screaming like some of the other's. They wave goodbye and I wave Noel over, hoping he sees me. He points me out to his teacher and I smile, Noel runs over and looks up at me expectantly.

"Hey." I smile. Unsure of what to say. *Why did younger kids make me so nervous?*

"Hi, you're Morgan, right?"

"Yup, Noel, right?" I wink and he laughs.

"Yes, can we go home today?"

"We can. There's no activities on the calendar." I took a photo on my phone so I double check. Tomorrow starts all the piano lessons, theater classes, and art classes.

"Awesome! Do you know how to play…" And all of a sudden we are best friends. Noel rambles off a thousand words a minute about this new game his mom got him and how excited he is to play. I tell him I've never played but I'm always down to learn. He's still talking by the time we get home that I almost forget to offer him a snack but Kayla's left us a note on the kitchen island.

'*Left a snack in the fridge for Noel, feel free to help yourself to anything else.*- Kayla'

At first, I'm not sure how it is going to be having her assistant here most of the time. She seems to be a little micro-managing but I think she has good intentions. She didn't seem to be like some of the other assistants I've come across in my life.

I pull out the plate of apple slices and peanut butter she left behind and realize I'll have to mention it to someone about my peanut allergy. It's not exactly some-thing you put on a job resume, but I guess if I am going to be living here it will be good for them to know.

"Hey, bud, Kayla left you some peanut butter and apples, but I'm incredibly allergic to peanuts so do you think I can make you something else?" I ask hopefully.

"Sure." He nods, taking a seat at the island.

"Okay, how do you feel about splitting a grilled cheese?" I ask, realizing I forgot to make myself something to eat in the chaos of the day.

"That sounds awesome!" He pauses. "But can you cut the crusts off? I don't like them." He frowns.

"Of course." I lean in close. "I don't like them either," I whisper. Looking around, I realize I'll have to do some snooping to figure out where everything is. *Well, is it snooping if you live here now?* Lucy's counters are bare with the exception of a fruit bowl so I get the impression she likes keeping things a certain way.

"The cheese is in the fridge," he says as if reading my mind.

"And the bread?"

"The cabinet." He points to the cabinet behind me.

I open it and find a loaf of white and wheat sitting on a shelf. I hold both up and Noel points to the white, I nod. It just tastes superior. Noel helps me find the frying pan and I grab some butter off the door of the fridge. He looks at me weird when I spread butter on either side of the bread before throwing it in the pan. It was the way my mother had always made it.

"You make grilled cheeses weird," Noel comments as he bites into his.

"But is it good?"

"Yeah, it's really good." He smiles and I laugh. *What had I been so nervous about?* Nannying seemed to be going well and day one was almost over.

I bite into my crustless grilled cheese and Noel pulls out a folder from his backpack. He starts working on what I assume is homework and I scroll on my phone aimlessly. There's a text from Lucy letting me know she'll be home by seven and to call not text if I have any issues. Noel finishes his sandwich and I do the dishes as he finishes up his homework. He's pretty quiet, all things considered, but I don't blame him. I wonder if it's weird for him to have nannies, let alone a brand new nanny suddenly.

"Can I play on my game now?" he asks, closing his folder.

"Is your homework done?"

"Most of it." He smiles and I see now these dimples are going to be a problem for me. This kid is cute as heck and knew it too.

"What's most of it?" I make a face.

"I just have to read for fifteen minutes." He shrugs.

"That's it? I love reading." I smile.

"I, uh, don't like it." He shifts uncomfortably. His mother runs a publishing company and the kid hates reading, talk about irony.

"Okay, how about this. We read for five minutes, then play for fifteen minutes and do that a few times until we make up those fifteen minutes?" I suggest.

"We can do that?" he asks excitedly.

"I don't see why not." I shrug. He smiles and grabs his book out of his backpack.

"I'll even go grab my book and we can read together on the couch." I smile.

"Okay!" He runs into the living room and I head to my room to grab my latest read **BLANK**. I just started it a few days ago and I am already loving it.

Noel takes a seat on one end of the couch with his little legs up, so I do the same on the other end. I set the timer on my phone for five minutes and we both start reading. Just as I'm getting invested the timer bings, which is kind of annoying, but Noel's never looked happier. He pulls out his gaming system and sets it up on the tv. I start the timer once the game starts and he plays his game. I read a bit while he's playing but it's a little distracting so I decide to wait until the designated reading time.

"Aw, man!" Noel frowns when the timer bings again. But he pauses the game and picks up his book without a second complaint. Those five minutes seem to fly by and he's back to playing again.

The last time, I get a little more protest from him. "Can't I just play one more time?" He looks at me with those baby blues but I stay strong.

"Nope, we're almost there." I encourage, and he pauses the game for the last time. Noel reads his book and when the timer goes off, he actually jumps up and cheers. I never knew someone could hate reading that much.

"Do you want to play?" Noel grabs a second controller and puts a new game in.

"I have no idea what to do but I can try," I admit.

Noel laughs but hands me the second controller. It's a game I recognize with the little plumber guy and the princess. He explains how the buttons work and decides I'm ready to go, I'm sure he just wants to win but he doesn't know how competitive I am. I'm focused on the screen trying to make my car go the right way and I slip on a banana that sends me spiraling. We're both cracking up at how bad I am at this game and I forget that I'm technically working. I know it is only my first day, but already I am enjoying my time here.

SIX

Lucy

I come home to the sound of laughter in the house. Which after the day I've had, is refreshing. Kicking off my heels and jacket, I find Morgan and Noel in the living room playing video games. They're both laughing and yelling at the tv about something but it's clear they're both having fun. I watch from the doorway, waiting for one of them to recognize I'm home. It is nice to come home to them having such a good time. A small part of me thinks about how nice it would be to come home to think every night. The love of my life and my son getting along so well. I only allow myself to consider that to be Morgan for the tiniest second before making my presence known.

"Mama!" Noel runs over for a hug and I smile.

"Hey, Miss Mars." Morgan smiles and I chuckle.

"You can call me Lucy." She's seen me naked, there is no need for formalities.

"Lucy." It falls off her lips like a melody.

"How was school, sweetie?" I ask Noel, trying to distract myself from the obvious attraction.

"It was okay." He shrugs.

"Did you want to go do your reading with me?" I ask, hoping for a better reaction than usual. I know he hates reading in his room by himself.

"I finished already!" he says proudly. I know it is only fifteen minutes of reading so I shouldn't be shocked, but if you know how those minutes usually go, you'd understand.

"Really?"

"Yeah! Morgan let me play games while I read." He says and I look at her confused.

"He means we set a timer, read in small increments, and took video game breaks in-between," she explains.

"Oh, well, that's fantastic then." I smile. *Why hadn't I thought of that?*

"We had dinner a little while ago, I made some chicken and pasta. There's some leftover, I made a plate because I wasn't sure if you've eaten." Morgan smiles.

"Thank you, I haven't actually." Unless you count the almonds I ate on the subway ride home. Which my growling stomach does not. I really should make more of an effort when it comes to dinner time.

"Why don't you go get ready for bed while I heat up my food?" I look at Noel. He nods and races to his room.

"So how was your first day?" Morgan follows me into the kitchen.

"It was good, Noel's a fun kid."

"Thank you," I say proudly.

"I wanted to mention something, it's small but maybe important?" Morgan shifts uncomfortably.

"Of course, what's going on?" I put the plate she left out for me in the microwave and press two minutes to start. I brace myself for what she's going to say. *Is she having a hard time with this because of last night? Is she quitting already?* I don't think I can go through the nanny process all over again, but I brace myself for whatever she's going to say.

"I'm pretty allergic to peanuts and Kayla had left out some peanut butter for Noel. I don't want to make any issues, I should've mentioned it but I can't really touch it or I break out in hives." She starts to ramble so I hold up a hand.

"Say no more. We'll have it taken care of. Noel can eat it out of the house, unless you're that allergic then we're happy to remove it completely."

"No, no. I just can't touch it, or give it to him myself," she explains.

"Then no problem." I pull out my phone. "I'm texting Kayla right now."

"Thank you." She smiles and I nod.

As I finish texting Kayla, I get an incoming phone call and excuse myself to my office. This was one of the reasons I had asked for soundproofing when we moved in. I had too many phone calls that I didn't need to be over-heard. Of course, at the time I didn't think it would be a call from my now ex-husband.

"What?" I answer angrily. I know before he speaks that I am going to be angry about this phone call.

"Wow, what a nice way to greet me," Kevin says snippily.

"Just get out with it, Kevin, I just got home." I sigh, sinking into my office chair.

"I was wondering if you could have Noel for Thanks-giving this year."

"Why?" I ask but I already know the answer. His new wife probably wants to go to another all inclusive resort that isn't kid friendly.

"Well, Demi wants to spend the holiday…"

"So you'd rather spend the weekend with your wife instead of your son? Again?" I say, cutting him off.

"I'll see him the next weekend. I mean your parents

probably want to see him anyway," he adds. He always does this, trying to act like he's doing me some kind of favor. It isn't that I don't want to have more time with Noel. I love that I will have him for Thanksgiving, but it is the fact that his father is dropping this into my lap *again*. That his father is bailing on him, *again*.

"Whatever. It's fine. But you better be here to get him this Friday night with no bullshit excuses," I growl.

"I'll be there," he mumbles, and I hang up before he can ask me about anything else. It is hard enough trying to coparent with him, but when he is so inconsistent, it makes my life inconsistent and I hate it. I am a fan of schedules and plans and notices, not last minute ditches. Besides it isn't fair to Noel when he is kept waiting on his days.

I leave a note for Kayla to not leave out anything peanuts for Morgan's sake, I know I texted her but I want to be sure she remembers. I feel so bad I didn't think to ask about allergies during the interview, considering she is living here. Kayla left me a pile of paperwork that I needed to get through tonight so I slump into my chair and try to make a dent into it. It is a busier time of year, choosing the books that will be published next year and finalizing the list for our higher ups. I don't mind it, but I will be happy when it is done in a few weeks and I have more time for Noel.

There's a knock on my office door and Morgan lets me know she has a plate of dinner for me. She walks inside with some kind of chicken and rice with a vegetable on a plate. My stomach growls instantly as it looks delicious.

"Thank you." I smile as she sets it on my desk.

"Noel said sometimes you forget to eat so I thought you might like something." Morgan smiles sheepishly.

"I do," I admit. "I appreciate it."

She nods and backs out of the room slowly. We were still trying to figure out how to maneuver around each other as boss and employee. I thought it would be harder but she seems to have packed up any residual feelings from our night together. I know I need to do the same, I just can't seem to shake it yet. She's the first woman I've been with since the divorce and it just seemed like the start of something new. I hadn't expected to see her as the only qualified person to be Noel's nanny.

I sigh and pull out the bottle of whiskey I keep on the bar in my office. Pouring myself a hearty glass, I dig into the dinner she made and sip my drink to calm my nerves. I need to get through this paperwork without thinking about my nanny in any other way than being my nanny.

After reading through three full manuscripts, I decide to call it a night. Noel and Morgan have already gone to bed a long time ago. I clean up my desk as best as I can and head to my room. I check on Noel first, kissing his forehead and pulling the blankets higher on him. Then I change into my pajamas and wonder how Morgan's sleeping. It must be weird to be staying in a new place. I decide it's not my place to check in on her but maybe I would ask tomorrow when I saw her.

I read a little before bed, one of the many books my publishing house, To Be Read Publishing, has published. But before long, the book is reading me and I'm falling asleep with the book falling next to me.

SEVEN

Morgan

Three weeks into being Noel's nanny, I start to get into the rhythm of things. I have the schedule memorized and we have a routine down for most things, which makes both of our lives easier. I had gone home for Thanksgiving last week while Noel and Lucy went to her parents' house in Florida for a few days, both of them coming back with beautiful tans. I am especially excited for today because it is Friday which means we have the weekend to go city exploring or do something that isn't educational. Which starts tonight with our new ritual of Friday night pizza. We bring it home so Lucy can have some and watch a movie together in the living room until Noel passes out on the couch and Lucy carries him to bed. We've only done it once but it is something I want to make a tradition.

Noel's extra happy when I pick him up from school today. He's talking a mile a minute on the way to grab the pizza. It had snowed overnight so the streets are covered in the black mush. You know the stuff that happens after five minutes of enjoying what snow should look like in the city. The brownstones are covered beautifully as are the bare trees but the streets are a mess. Every year it is one of those things I hate about the winter.

"Hey, Noel," a kid calls behind us in line for pizza.

"Hey, Nash!" Noel smiles and the two boys get into a conversation that any grown up would get lost in. Nash's mom/nanny stands closer to me and smiles.

"Hi, I'm Tammy." She holds out her hand.

"Morgan. I'm Noel's Nanny," I offer, hoping she might explain who she is.

"Oh! You must be the new nanny. Nash and Noel have had playdates but I usually schedule them with Vera."

"Yes, I just started a few weeks ago."

"I'm Nash's mom, by the way, I realize I didn't say that." She pushes back her blonde hair with her manicured hand and I can't help but notice she's not wearing a wedding ring. She is attractive, not as hot as Lucy but for a mom, she is definitely a MILF. I'm not sure when Lucy became the standard of attractiveness for me, but I try not to think too much about that.

"It's nice to meet you."

"Did you boys want to eat together?" Tammy asks them. Noel looks at me and I nod. I am a little disappointed we won't be eating with Lucy but some nights she has already eaten without us anyway.

"Sounds good. I can grab the pizza if you want to grab a table?" Tammy suggests with a smile.

"Sure." I nod. The boys run to the back and pick out a table together. Taking a seat at the two person table next to them, Tammy sits across from me and passes out the pizza.

"So how'd you end up as a nanny?" Tammy asks as she takes a handful of napkins to remove the pizza grease from her slice. Personally, I think that's the best part of the pizza. If it's not dripping all over you, then where's the fun. But I also think that about my women.

"I was looking for a new job to finish paying for college. It kind of fell into my lap," I admit. Just like Noel's mom did.

"Oh! You're in college, that's so awesome. What are you going to school for?"

"I'm an education major, I'm thinking about becoming a teacher." I smile.

"That's wonderful, such an under appreciated career," she says and I don't know if she means it as a compliment or an insult.

"What do you do?" I ask.

"Oh, I'm a stay at home mom. I used to model back in the day," she says proudly. "Wow, that's amazing," I praise.

"I miss it sometimes, but my son is my life and I wouldn't have it any other way," she adds. The boys are deep into their pizza and their own conversation.

Tammy goes on to ask me more about myself and a little part of me feels like this is some kind of setup. I know Noel wouldn't do anything like that, but I wouldn't put it past Tammy. From what I see, she is beautiful but she is smart too. So when she asks me out at the end of our pizza date, I'm not surprised.

"What do you say? We can grab a real dinner one night without the kiddos?"

"Sure." I smile. I'm not one to turn down a free meal.

"Does tomorrow night work?"

"I think so, I'll have to double check with Lucy but it shouldn't be an issue." She had said I could have nights off, although I hadn't used any yet. *Do I need to tell her it is so I could go on a date?* I don't know why that suddenly feels like I am cheating on her.

"Oh Lucy loves me, here's my number and I can pick you up at eight." Tammy hands me a card before taking Nash with her.

"Where are you going with Nash's mom?" Noel asks, looking at the card confused.

"I think on a date," I blurt out before I can think about it. Surely Noel knew about two women dating, right? I mean his mom is clearly some kind of queer. He just shrugs as we leave the pizza place so I guess he knows. Thank goodness, that isn't something I'd want to have to explain.

We go back to Noel's apartment and Lucy is there waiting for us. Dressed in her pjs, which consist of an oversized Columbia sweatshirt and leggings. She isn't on the phone for a change and greets Noel with a hug.

"You're home!" He cheers happily.

"I thought we could have a movie night? I was about to make some popcorn." She smiles.

"That sounds awesome!"

"Great, go change into some pjs." Noel races down the hall to his room. I take off my boots and winter coat, hanging up Noel's that he left on the ground.

"You're welcome to join us," Lucy offers.

"That's okay, I was actually going to catch up on some reading, if that's okay?" I appreciate the offer but I had a long week and am dying to rest a bit. Plus I am in the middle of a really good book I have been wanting to get back to all day.

"Of course, but feel free to join us if that book gets boring." She winks, and I feel my stomach doing summersaults that I wish would stop.

"Thank you." I chuckle. "So, I was wondering if I could get tomorrow off?"

"Sure, that shouldn't be a problem." She smiles. "Big date?" she asks with a slight laugh and I pause awkwardly. "Oh."

"I-I don't have to go," I mumble.

"No, of course you can have a dating life. I just request you not bring anyone back here…for Noel, of course," she adds.

"Of course. I wouldn't dream of it." I nod. That thought hadn't even crossed my mind. We pause awkwardly for a moment until I head to my room. Noel's racing out on the way, dressed in his Spiderman pjs.

I wish it wasn't so awkward with Lucy. There are times when I could see us becoming friends, her letting her guard down and then it comes to a screeching halt like tonight. I don't know what's worse, hoping we can be friends or living in a house with someone that's basically a stranger. I decide not to think about it and change into some comfortable clothes, sliding underneath the warm covers and opening my book.

I can hear laughter coming from the living room, Lucy and Noel's as they watch their movie. It is sweet, I don't remember laughing that much with my parents when I was a kid. Not that they didn't spend time with me, I'm sure they did. But they were quieter and more laid back when it came to parenting then Lucy is with Noel. It is nice to witness, even though she works a lot she is still around where it counts.

I think about Tammy and I realize I haven't texted her yet. I climb out of bed and dig through my jeans for her card, pulling out my phone and send her a quick text letting her know I am on for tomorrow. I don't really feel excited about it but maybe that is a good thing, less of a chance for getting hurt.

It's after midnight when I wake up with my book open next to me and drool on my pillow. Wiping the side of my mouth, I get out of bed with a stretch and decide to sneak to the kitchen for a snack. I had the pizza so many hours ago, I am in the mood for a little something. Hopefully I can make something without waking anyone else up. I tiptoe to the kitchen and find Lucy leaning over the counter. Her perfect ass on display in the tightest of leggings as she makes something.

"Lucy?" I whisper but she doesn't turn around. She's bobbing her head lightly as if listening to music with some kind of beat.

"Holy shit!" she yelps as she spins around and sees me. She pulls out her AirPods and holds her chest.

"I'm sorry, I said your name."

"You can't go around spooking old ladies, I'm not as young as I used to be," she teases.

"You are in no way an old lady." I scoff.

"Well, thank you." She smiles. "What are you doing up?"

"I could ask you the same thing."

"Yes, but this is my house," she says with a smirk.

"I was hungry," I admit.

"Me too, no one brought me home any pizza this week."

"Hey, sometimes you're not even home."

"A lady always likes coming home to pizza." Lucy laughs.

"Okay, I'll remember that for next time."

"Want some hot cocoa? I just made some. It always helps me when I can't sleep."

"That sounds great." I nod. I can't remember the last time I had a cup of hot cocoa.

"Why can't you sleep?" I whisper in the quiet.

"Oh you know, just a million things on my mind." She waves her hands in the air as if to say it's no big deal.

"Do you want to talk about it?"

"Oh, I'm sure my shrink can handle it." I can't tell if she's joking or not. She picks up a k-cup and puts it into the coffee machine.

"I'm serious, we can talk about it if you want to." I don't want to push her but I also feel bad if she's having so much trouble sleeping.

"I just worry about Noel and his father. He's not seeing him as much as he used to, especially since he got remarried. I wonder how it's affecting him," she says with a sigh. The Keurig machine makes a sound as the water begins to pour into the cup.

"You'd never know it from talking to him," I say honestly.

"Really?"

"Your son is so incredibly happy and loved. He talks about you all the time and you making time for him, quality time is so well received."

"That's such a relief, sometimes I wonder if I'm doing enough for him." She frowns as she hands me the mug.

I reach out to touch her hand lightly. "You're doing more than enough, don't beat yourself up over it." Lucy glances down at our hands and I pull back, blushing. I hadn't meant to make it so intimate.

"Sorry—"

"No, it's okay. I should be getting back to bed. Thank you." She avoids eye contact as she grabs her AirPods, her hot cocoa, and quietly walks back to her room. Leaving me even more confused about how I feel about her.

EIGHT

Lucy
___

Morgan walks out for her date with Tammy and I'm clenching my jaw so tight, it almost gets locked. It isn't that I was jealous of them. I know I'm not. That would be crazy. It has already been weeks since we hooked up and neither of us has made it weird. Granted, we don't spend too much time together, and when we do Noel is around. But still, I definitely am not having feelings for her. Morgan hadn't mentioned who the date was with but Noel had mentioned it casually when asking for a playdate with Nash last night. We had watched a few holiday movies before he passed out on the couch and I carried him to bed.

Morgan and I hadn't spoken since last night. I hadn't meant to make things weird but after she touched my hand and I got a physical chill down my spine, I knew we were headed to dangerous territory. She is my nanny, for Christ's sake, and Noel was sleeping right down the hall. I couldn't afford to have any kind of reaction like that with someone who I should only be seeing professionally.

"I shouldn't be back too late, and I have my key so I'll

be quiet when I come in," she says as she picks up her purse.

"No worries. I have work to do so I might be up anyway," I say with a smile. Morgan nods and heads out the door.

I wish I could say her leaving made focusing on my work easier, but it didn't. Noel is in the living room playing his new video game. I sit with him for a bit but my mind can't leave the thought of Morgan hooking up with Tammy. It isn't that I have an issue with Tammy. But the thought of Morgan touching anyone else the way she touched me has me more jealous than I've ever been. I know I have no right to be, so I go to my office and try reading over the new manuscripts Becca left in my inbox.

But as I try to read the books, I can only imagine Morgan as the main love interests. A nanny- boss love story that seems to be a little too real right now, a one night stand turned lovers and a single mom rom-com makes these feel too personal. Is Becca or someone in the office playing a joke on me? It is nothing against these writers, the writing is fantastic, but I can't look at any of them objectively right now. I'll have to have Dylan look these over for me instead and give me the basic notes.

As it gets later and later, I try not to think about Morgan and what she might be up to. I put Noel to bed with extra books and later than normal to give me something to distract myself. I can't help but wait up for her since it is already past ten. At this point, the curiosity is killing me and I need to at least know how the date went. I know it is crazy and truly none of my business, but I can't help myself. I'm sitting on the couch pretending to read a book when I hear the key turn in the lock. Morgan's tiptoeing to her room when she sees me sitting in the living room with the lamp on.

"Oh, hey." She smiles, leaning on the doorway.

"Hey, how was your night?" I ask nonchalantly. I don't know what it is about this woman that gets me so worked up.

"Honestly? It was pretty terrible," she says with a laugh. Relief rushes through my bones.

"Want to talk about it?" I ask, repeating the words she said to me last night.

"You don't want to hear about this, do you?" she says, unsure.

"It's that or I get back to my book." I shrug.

"Okay, well, I won't leave you hanging then. Let me go change first." I nod and she heads to her room. A few minutes later she comes out with her hair in a bun on the top of her head, dressed in flannel pjs and no makeup. It isn't the first time I've seen her like this but it is still amazing to watch as she is equally as beautiful. She is effortlessly beautiful.

"So, what happened?" I prompt. She takes a seat on the other side of the couch, putting her knees to her chest and looks at me, letting out a big sigh.

"She was SO boring," she exasperates.

"Really? What is her name?" I ask, playing dumb.

"Tammy? I don't know her last name. Nash's mom." She sighs.

"Oh, I should've warned you. That woman is a different breed."

"I wish you would have." She chuckles. "She didn't stop talking about herself all night."

"Let me guess, about her modeling days?" I have been forced into too many conversations about how she gave up her modeling career to be a full time mom.

"Look, I'm fine to listen to anyone talk about their past,

but if I can't get a word in edgewise then why did she even invite me out?" She sighs.

"Maybe she was trying to impress you?" I offer.

"No, because I swear when she wasn't talking about herself she was talking just to hear her own voice."

"What do you mean?"

"She just kept commenting on everything and it was so negative. Like I'm not the most positive person in the world, but holy shit everything she said was like '*ugh this tastes gross, don't they know how to cook or were they raised by someone without tastebuds?*'" Morgan mocks Tammy's voice so well that I laugh out loud.

"That was a perfect impression."

"Well, I heard enough of her voice." She chuckles.

"So no second date?" I joke.

"I wouldn't even kiss her at the end of the night. Her mouth had been too busy I doubt she even noticed." A second wave of relief.

"How did you end the night then?"

"I lied and said you needed me early tomorrow morning so I had to get home," she says shyly.

"You used Noel and I?!" I gasp jokingly.

"I didn't know how else to get out of it! She was trying to get me to go back to her place. I knew it would be a tour of her past modeling days and I was already falling asleep."

"You're so bad." I push my hand forward to touch hers playfully and she laughs.

"You seemed to like that about me," she says with a glimmer in her eye. Instinctively, I'm biting my bottom lip and hating that her words went right to my pussy.

"Morgan," I say warningly. But I don't know if it is more of a warning to her or myself.

"Don't worry, I'm done dating for now. I like being

single too much. It will take someone special to get this gal to settle down." She locks eyes with me and I swear it is her way of saying that could be me. But no, it can't be. She is the *nanny*. *My* nanny.

"I should get to bed," I say, suddenly feeling too seen.

"Me too." Morgan smiles and we both head our separate ways for the night.

NINE

Morgan

Things have been a little awkward between Lucy and I since I went out with Tammy. If I didn't know better, I'd say she was actually jealous I went out with someone else. Then we shared this moment that was flirty as hell but I didn't know what it meant. She is all kinds of mixed signals and I don't know what to do with them. It is like she isn't sure what she wants with me. I decide to ask Ellie about it. She has a lot more experiences with this kind of thing than I do. I am more of the one night stand type, where Ellie is the one who has women falling in love with her everywhere she goes.

Lucy has taken Noel to the Museum of Natural History for the day so I am on my own. Which feels weird as I am walking to the subway. I keep looking back as if I have forgotten someone or something. Ellie meets me at our favorite brunch spot uptown, the Sunflour cafe.

"Damn, you look so cute!" I praise Ellie, she is somehow always dressed up to the latest fashion trends despite living off an assistant's salary and paying for college like me.

"Oh, this lil thing?" She spins, showing off her new coat and black dress with white polka dots. They compliment her bright pink hair perfectly and show off her curves.

"You're too much." I laugh rolling my eyes.

We both sit and order right away, her gluten free salad and my BLT on sourdough. Sometimes we try new things but today I want something familiar.

"So, what did you need to talk about?"

"I think I have feelings for my boss," I admit aloud.

"You what?" She almost spits out her water.

"I'm not saying it again," I say firmly.

"Okay, but this is big. You're like me, you don't go around catching feelings for people." She is right; she, Bella and I are three people who don't go around falling for people easily, we have up walls and boundaries so this doesn't happen. Then again, even if Bella doesn't want to admit it, there is definitely something going on between her and Lucy's co-worker.

"I know." I sigh. The food arrives and we eat in silence as Ellie thinks of what to say next.

"So you like her, can you do anything about it?"

"About a week ago I would've said no. But ever since I went out with someone else, she's been like super flirty and I can't tell where we stand. It's almost like she's upset with me for going out."

"From a boss's standpoint or a jealous ex?"

"Definitely a jealous ex."

"Ugh, this is why I do one night stands and not call the next day. This is so overly complicated for no reason," I grumble into my fries.

"I've never seen you this bent out of shape about someone," Ellie says taking a bite of her salad.

"I just like her, and I like her kid too. He's smart and

fun, it's not a bad job at all." I try not to think about how this is all temporary.

"What are you going to do when the job ends? Couldn't you wait and ask her out then?"

"I didn't really think about that," I admit. I've been so focused on not thinking about when it ends that I never considered Lucy and I having a chance after I'm not her employee. Then we aren't breaking any rules and if she turns me down I will never have to see her again. I ignore the thought of how much that hurts.

"There you go. Then you have time to come out with us for New Year's Eve. Bella says she might be missing it."

"What? We always go out." It is one of those days where we dress in skimpy clothes and get free drinks handed to us all night. It is like my own version of Christmas.

"I know, but she might have a holiday party with your boss." Ellie shrugs. I'll have to talk to Bella and see what is up with her lately.

After brunch, Ellie and I head our separate ways. I call Bella on the way home but she doesn't pick up so I leave a voicemail asking her to call me. When I get home for the day, Lucy and Noel are still out. So I retreat to my room and do something I haven't been able to in weeks. Scratch an itch that desperately needs to be scratched. I pull out my smallest and quietest vibrator from my nightstand and set it on the bed. I light a candle because I like to set the mood and climb under my sheets.

I pull up a video of two women and put the vibrator on

my clit on the lowest setting. As the video heats up and I get wetter, I slide two fingers inside myself. Closing my eyes, I can hear the moans coming from the video and I pretend they're Lucy's.

"Oh, Lucy," I whisper moan as I pump my fingers in and out of my core. I am fucking soaked for her. Thinking about the night we spent together is enough for me to throw my phone aside.

My vibrator doesn't leave my clit as I think about how beautiful she looks naked. How incredibly tight and fit she is, how perky and round her breasts are. Just big enough to need two hands to hold them. Her taut pink nipples and the way her bare pussy was dripping for me. I moan her name again and I can feel my orgasm building. I've never come this fast before but I've never thought about someone like this either.

"Ohh," I audibly gasp as I add a third finger and just like that, my legs are shaking and I'm coming to the thought of the one woman I can't have.

I sigh, shutting off the women moaning and walking to the bathroom to clean my toy. I always thought it was weird that they refer to sex things as toys but then again, it is something you have a lot of fun with. I carefully tuck it back in it's hiding spot and look for some clothes to get dressed into. It is chilly in here so I opt for some leggings and a sweater. It's when I open my door I'm met with Lucy standing before me with her hand extended like she wants to knock.

"Oh!" My eyes widen. *How long has she been standing there?*

"We, umm, just got back. I wanted to see if you needed anything?" she asks, clearing her throat.

"No, thank you, I was just coming to get some water." Poor word choice on my part but Lucy's face is unreadable. So if she did hear me, she isn't showing that she did.

"Okay, Noel's playing his game so I'll be in my office for a bit if you can keep an eye on him?"

"Sure." I smile.

"Thanks." She doesn't say anything else but leaves my door open as she goes. I grab my phone, my book, and find Noel in the living room.

"Hey, Mom said you might be napping."

"Nope, I'm awake." I clench my jaw, wondering if again if Lucy had heard something.

"Want to play a game?" he asks, holding out the controller.

"Sure." I nod. I'm not any good at this game but I think Noel just likes having someone else to play with. I don't blame him, I had grown up as an only child and it was pretty lonely.

TEN

Lucy

I open the front door and I'm less than thrilled to see my ex-husband standing before me. He is a half an hour late which means I will be late for my night. But at least he is here, that's what I'm supposed to be happy about, right?

"Noel! Your father is here!" I call and he comes running down the hall.

"Daddy!" He clings to his father's legs and I clench, wondering if he'd be as happy to see him if he knew how much it took to get him here. Sometimes it is hard being the only parent in this relationship.

"Noel! You forgot your backpack." Morgan walks down the hallway holding the bag we helped him pack. Full of clothes and things I'm not sure Kevin had any of.

"Who's this?" Kevin asks, crushing his eyebrows together. I know what he is thinking, it isn't a secret I am bisexual. It is something that used to make him crazy jealous so I relish in this for a moment before answering.

"This is Noel's new nanny, Morgan."

"What happened to Vera?" he asks. But I know what

he's saying, what happened to the less attractive, older, pregnant woman?

"She left to have her baby."

"Nice to meet you." Morgan reaches to shake Kevin's hand and I hold back a smirk as best I can.

"Yeah." He shakes back unwillingly. "Let's go, bud."

"Bye, Noel, I'll see you Sunday night." I bend down to hug Noel and give him a kiss on my head. He surprises us all by stopping to hug Morgan too.

"All right, all right." Kevin ushers him out the door and I laugh.

"What was that all about?" Morgan asks.

"My ex husband probably being jealous I hired the hot nanny," I say with a laugh. Morgan blushes and I realize what I've said but it's too late to take it back. I mean it isn't a secret, Morgan is beautiful.

"Shit, I'm late." I glance at my watch and head to my room. I am supposed to be out of here in an hour and I still haven't showered.

I quickly rinse off, washing my hair and blow drying it just as quickly. I'm racing around my room in just a towel, trying to find my dress and shoes I had picked out earlier in the week. I curl my hair and add a thin layer of makeup to my face. I slide on my green velvet dress and realize I can't zip up the back. I reach a few different ways, thankful for my flexibility, but it's no use. This is something they don't warn you about being single. You can open pickle jars fine but zipping up dresses is where the real problem is.

"Morgan?" I open my door a crack and peek out to call her name.

"Yes?" She pops her head out from the kitchen.

"Can you come help me?"

"Sure." She looks at me weird but comes to help. I

open the door more and show her how the dress won't close.

"I can't get it on my own." I sigh.

"Oh, no problem." She smiles and I turn around, showing her my exposed back. This isn't the kind of dress you wear a bra with, so I am basically naked except for a small pair of lace panties.

Her hands are warm as she reaches for the zipper. It feels like minutes pass as she slowly drags the zipper up the length of my back. I can feel the hesitation in her fingertips as she closes it.

"There's a small clasp at the top too," she says and I nod. She carefully pulls my curls to one side of neck and her fingers gently brush over my neck, causing me to shudder.

"Your hands are so warm," I notice aloud.

"I was drinking a hot coffee," she explains and I nod again.

She finishes moving my hair to the side and I can feel her breath on my neck. I know it's not on purpose but a blush creeps across my cheeks as I think about the last time we were this close. A flood of emotions rush through me was I recall that night in vivid detail. Morgan connects the clasp and I turn around to face her, straightening out my dress.

"How do I look?" I ask.

"Beautiful, so beautiful." She smiles and I can feel the tension between us growing stronger. It is like a scene in a movie, the one right before we'd kiss for the first time. Well, for the second, first time.

She reaches for my hair, this time to place it over my back. Her warm fingertips brushing against my cheek and I close my eyes falling into her hand. *What are we doing?* I open my eyes and she's looking into mine. As if to say, *now what?* This is what drives me wild about her, I never know the answer. Sometimes all I want is a plan, a perfectly devised solution of how to act around her. She keeps me on my toes and I surprisingly don't hate it.

"Morgan," I whisper softly but she doesn't speak. Instead she leans in close enough to make me think she's about to kiss me. But then her hands are touching my neck with something cool. I open my eyes and realize she's putting on my necklace carefully so my hair doesn't get caught in it. Just like that all the tension is gone and I can think clearly again.

"You're all set." She smiles and I nod.

"Thank you."

She ducks out of my room and it gives me a moment to relax. I don't want to show up to a party for my own company with a new batch of wrinkles. I take three deep breaths and slip on my heels before grabbing my purse. It's small enough to fit my lipstick and my phone but not big enough to hold anything else.

"Noel's with his dad so I don't think you'll need anything but if you do, my cell is on," I tell Morgan as I stop in the kitchen on the way out. She is in the middle of making some kind of dinner and it smells delicious.

"Okay, I'll probably just be in my room reading or reeling over finishing the last Colleen Hoover book." She chuckles.

"You're a Hoover fan?" I ask surprised.

"Yeah, her books are like my guilty pleasure, don't tell anyone," she says with a wink. I laugh and make a point to stop at my office before heading out. Grabbing something off my shelf, I sneak into Morgan's room and palace it on her nightstand.

I'm only fifteen minutes late thanks to an Uber driver that didn't know what "drive faster" meant. But by the way my boss is looking at me you'd think I forgot to put on pants. He's across the room, talking to someone that's trying to get his attention, but he manages to shoot me a warning glare. I don't enjoy having a boss, if I am being honest, and I know I know, who does? But this is different, Dylan and I could essentially run the publishing house on our own but about a year ago the board thought it would be a good idea to hire someone as our superior. We tried to fight it to no avail, so now some twenty-two year old that knows less about our company than we do is in charge. Which means he cares more about appearances and parties than the actual work we do.

"I saw our boss gave you a look, I thought you might need this." Dylan walks over, handing me a martini.

"I just know he's going to come over and say something." I sigh, taking a hearty sip.

"Just say you were having a family emergency with that hot nanny of yours," she teases, but my cheeks turn ten shades of red.

"Oh my gosh! Was there actually something going on!?" she squeals and I remind her to shush.

"No." I shake my head. Whatever our moment was earlier, it didn't need to be dissected by my best friend. I want to keep it between us. *Whatever it is.*

"Mmm huh," she says, unconvinced.

"So, you ladies have time to gossip but not to show up on time?" Tony, our boss, says sassily.

"Well, I had an emergency with the nanny," I lie.

"See I don't buy that, but it doesn't matter to me. Just get on talking with more potential donors, we can use all the help we can get." He downs his champagne, throwing his head back, and forces a fake smile.

"He's got to get that stick out of his ass removed," Dylan whispers, and I giggle.

But Dylan's attention turns as she looks at the woman across the room. Dressed in a scarlet red, strapless dress she commands the attention of every man and woman in the room. She was young, probably in her twenties. She makes her way across the room and that's when I notice Dylan looking nervous.

"That's my date," she says and my jaw drops. It's not that Dylan isn't beautiful, she is gorgeous. But I didn't know she liked women. She's exclusively brought a lot of shitty guys to these kind of things. You know, the kind who don't even have their own suits. So I am shocked when this bombshell is walking toward us.

"Lucy, this is Bella. Bella, this is Lucy." She introduces herself and Bella throws her arms around me like we're old friends.

"Thank you so much for getting my best friend the job, she absolutely adores Noel." Bella smiles. Now I am even more confused, this is Bella? I thought Bella was some kind of paid worker, she doesn't look like one. Not that there is a specific type, but I guess I had it in my head that she was someone else entirely.

"I'm glad, I love her working for us," I say honestly. She makes the house more of a home than my other nannies ever did.

"We should go mingle," Dylan says shyly and Bella nods.

"Nice meeting you." She smiles and I can't help but

notice Dylan's hand on her ass as they walk away. I am going to be incredibly confused about their relationship until the end of time. But as long as my best friend is happy, I don't care. Now if only I could find that for myself too.

ELEVEN

Morgan

After I finish putting Noel to bed, I clean up a bit. Tidying his toys and doing the dishes, just the little things to make the house less messy before Lucy comes home. I end the night climbing into my bed but something on my nightstand catches my eye. It's a book but not one that I recognize, and across the side says *Advanced Reader Copy*. Where had this come from? I'm about to text Lucy and make sure she didn't misplace something when I realize it might be for me. I pick it up gently even though it's clearly just a book. There's no note or anything but I open the inside and realize this is from one of my favorite authors and it's a book that hasn't even been announced yet.

Lucy must've remembered that she was my favorite and left it here for me to read. Kat Savage was one of my first indie authors that I had ever picked up. There are so many amazing, lesser known writers who are only now starting to get noticed. I dive into her new book, excited to be taken into whichever world she's written. I truly haven't picked up a book of hers that I haven't liked yet.

Page after page, I'm completely devouring the book

whole. I know I'll be exhausted in the morning but I don't care. I *have* to know how this book ends. It is about a single mom finding love with someone unexpected and I am eating it up. Of course, I recognize the similarities to Lucy and I within the pages. Had she done that on purpose? Clearly she read it before I did.

I'm about to finish reading when I hear the front door click closed. It is quiet but I can hear the click clack of Lucy's heels until she reaches her room. I hear Noel's door open, probably to check on him and then I hear her in the hallway. Instead of pretending to sleep, I decide to be bold and walk out.

"Oh! You're still up," Lucy says surprised.

"Yeah, I was reading," I say with a smile, holding up the book. "How is it?" She smiles.

"I love it. Thank you so much," I gush.

"She's incredibly talented. She got signed with us a few months ago but I couldn't say anything until the contract was finalized," she explains.

"I'm so excited."

"Do you think you could help me with my dress again?" She points to the zipper and I nod.

I put the book down on the table in the hall and follow her into her room. She closes the door behind us and I give her a look, but she says "Just so Noel doesn't wake up."

I nod and wait as she takes off her jacket, hangs it in the closet, and I try not to think about the last time I was in here. Just a few hours ago she had been so flirty and it seemed like we were about to kiss. Part of me wonders if that is what she has in mind now. Suddenly I feel like a school girl with a first crush.

"Can you help?" She stands in front of me and I unzip her quicker than I had earlier. I don't want to tempt fate twice.

"D-Do you want some hot cocoa?" I blurt out randomly. *Where had that come from?*

"Uh, sure." She looks at me weird but I dash out of there before she can say anything else.

I make my way to the kitchen, grabbing my book on the way out. I place two k-cups on the counter and turn on the machine. This time I grab some mini marshmallows and wait for the machine to heat up. A few minutes later, a naked faced Lucy takes a seat at the island while I make the hot cocoas.

"Thank you." She smiles, but as I hand her the cup our fingers brush together and I drop the cup. Hot cocoa spilling everywhere and a loud crash as the cup hits the floor.

"Shit, I'm so sorry," I whisper.

"It's okay, it happens. Let me grab the glass, you're barefoot." I try to step over the mess but I accidentally step into a piece of glass and end up jumping in pain, which makes me bump my hip into the counter.

"I'm a mess," I mumble aloud as I take a seat on the ground. It is safe on the floor and I hold my foot up to look at the damage. I definitely have a piece wedged in there.

"What's going on?" Noel comes out sleepy eyed, yawning.

"I'm sorry, bud, Morgan and I dropped a cup." Lucy frowns.

"I'm sorry," I whisper.

"It's okay, just get back to bed." Noel nods and heads back to his room. Lucy finishes cleaning up the mess and checks her slippers for any glass before coming to help me.

"I'm fine, really. If you could grab me the tweezers I can get it out myself."

"Morgan, just let me help." She sits down next to me and taps on her leg. I place my foot on the spot and she takes a look. "It's in there pretty deep. Can you walk or should I bring stuff here?"

"I-I can walk," I say unsteadily. So much for wanting to impress Lucy. That dream has clearly gone out the window.

"Okay." She helps me up and I limp with her to her room. She walks me into her bathroom and sits me on the toilet.

"Put your foot on the tub," she instructs. Then she continues looking through her medicine cabinet for supplies. She pulls out a few things and sits on the edge of the bathtub, placing my foot on her lap and starts with the alcohol.

"It's going to hurt, but it needs to be cleaned." I nod and try not to wince as she cleans it. Then she gets the tweezers and I don't look. But she holds out one hand and I squeeze gently. It hurts a lot but I am trying not to let on.

"There." She holds up a rather large piece of glass in the air with the tweezers and I can feel relief in my foot. She must have gotten it all.

"Thank you." I smile. She nods and reaches behind me to throw it in the garbage. As she sits back down, our faces are only inches apart. She hesitates for a moment and I steady her with my hands on her waist as she pushes a piece of hair out of my eyes. I think we're about to kiss when we hear footsteps approaching. She pulls away just as quickly to put a bandaid on my foot as Noel steps into the bathroom.

"Mom? Can you tuck me in again?" Noel asks.

"Of course." She pauses to look at me. "You okay?"

"Yes." I smile and she leaves, the moment passing between us just as quickly.

"We're decorating for Christmas?" I ask surprised when I wake up the next morning. It is a Monday but a snow day so Noel stayed home. Lucy decided to work from home since the roads are so bad, but now that it is an acceptable time to leave work she has pulled out the Christmas boxes from the hall closet.

"Of course! It's already December," she says as if it's obvious. My family had never been big on decorating so I am surprised is all.

"Decorating the tree is my favorite," Noel says proudly as he begins digging in the boxes.

"Well, what can I do to help?" My foot is still killing me but I don't want to be unhelpful.

"No, your job is to park it on that couch and rest your foot," Lucy says firmly.

"But-"

"You know I'm right." She shoots me a look and I sigh. *What is it about this woman?*

"I know." I sigh and take a seat on the couch.

I watch as Noel and Lucy start unboxing their decorations. There are loads of nutcrackers, snowmen, and Santa clauses that I don't think will fit, even in this sizable apartment. Noel is running around with all the toys that sing and dance when you press a button while Lucy is actually decorating. It is hard not to look at her, she looks so graceful as she hangs up stocking and the ornaments balls all around the living room. I also notice how nice her ass looks in the jeans she is wearing and how she apparently has a small lower back tattoo. Whenever she stands on her tippy toes to reach something, her sweater will lift just

67

enough to tease me. I am dying to know what it is. I am a sucker for some lower back art. The first time we had sex it was so dark at my apartment, I must not have noticed it.

"We need some music!" Lucy exclaims and turns on the speaker. Out blasts some Pop Christmas music, and she and Noel start dancing around the living room. She twirls him and he jumps, dancing around the decorations. I get into the spirit, bopping my head as much as I can from the couch.

"We have a job for you." Lucy walks over with a handful of garland. "We need that untangled, please," she says with a giggle.

"Uh, this seems more like a punishment." I raise an eyebrow. "Maybe my foot hurts more than I thought," I joke.

"Good thing you have two hands that work." She winks and I clench my jaw. This woman is teasing me surely.

I start untangling the garland while she continues dancing around the room. She is like a mom straight out of a Christmas movie with how much she likes it. Noel puts up the nutcrackers along the bookshelves and I realize she has an overabundance of them. Each one looks different, one is dressed like Dunkin donuts, one has a stack of books, and one has a coffee cup in hand and a phone in the other. It is kind of cute, each one marked with the year they came out.

"Do you collect those?" I ask Lucy.

"I used to," she says with a sigh.

"She used to buy one every year, they're her favorite," Noel says happily.

"What made you stop?"

"Running out of room," she says with a laugh.

"I untangled half but I think I need some help," I say

hopefully. I am so tired of the twisting and pulling of the garland, it is extremely intricate.

"Wow, you did that quick. I can never get it. Every year we just throw it back in the box," she teases and I frown.

"You mean I didn't need to do that?" I deadpan.

"Well, you did! Thank you." She blows me a kiss after first making sure Noel isn't looking and I blush profusely. *Did she just blow me a kiss? What the hell did that mean?*

She walks over to the box, looks around for something, and pulls out a small piece of mistletoe. Lucy gives me a look and then walks over to the living room entrance, pulls out the step ladder, and tries to hang it.

"Can you give me a hand?" she asks and I look at her confused.

"Sure." I stand up, unsure of how much help I can be while I'm limping.

"Just be sure to catch me if I fall," she instructs so I stand behind her, ready for us both to go falling. Then she hangs the mistletoe with no problem, gets down, and looks at me. I'm about to ask what she's doing when Noel jumps up.

"Ew! You're both under the mistletoe, that means you have to kiss!" He covers his eyes and before I have a chance to react, Lucy's pressing her lips against mine.

TWELVE

Lucy

I don't know what came over me, but I knew it would be the perfect chance to kiss Morgan again. I've been dying to for weeks but lately the hunger has gotten stronger and stronger. I've always been a fan of Christmastime, something about the lights and the time of year brings out this joy in me. I also love watching Noel light up as we decorate the house together, it is one of my favorite traditions.

"Ew!" Noel exclaims as Morgan and I pull apart.

"Oh, hush!" I shake my head as if what we did is no big deal. I don't make it a habit to go kissing the nanny in front of him. Well, kissing anyone in front of him. But he looks more bothered at the act of catching cooties from kisses than the fact that I was kissing a woman, or his nanny.

Morgan takes a seat back on the couch and begins untangling the lights again. Her cheeks are as red as Santa's sleigh and she is avoiding eye contact with me. I am glad I finally did something to keep her on her toes. It is rare I get a chance to do that.

We go back to decorating like what just happened is

the most normal thing. Noel and I are dancing around the room, hanging the lights Morgan's untangling, and it's hard not to imagine this is how it could always be. How easy life could be with the three of us. I don't know if that is something she'll even want, she is so hard to read lately. But with the way she is looking at me, I know I need to find out.

"Mom, what time am I going to Nash's house?" My jaw clenches at the thought of Tammy and Morgan's date until I remember what a train wreck it was.

"Six," Morgan answers for me, having his schedule memorized.

"Awesome! Can I bring the new game you bought me?"

"Only if you're super careful," I warn.

"I will, I will." He groans.

Noel goes back to rearranging the nutcrackers and I realize tonight would be the perfect chance to make my move. Noel won't be home and we'll have the house to ourselves, maybe we'll have the chance to talk about what is going on between us. I know it isn't all in my head, not after the way she's been looking at me. I just need the perfect way to start a conversation, and as Noel places the last nutcracker on the shelf, it hits me.

Morgan takes Noel to his sleepover so it gives me an opportunity to find the perfect book off my shelf to leave on her bedside. I'm not the best at communicating exactly how I am feeling, especially with Morgan. But giving her a book that will open the gates to talking seems like the perfect opportunity for us. Last night after Noel went to bed we talked about the book for hours, how much she liked it, the themes and how relatable it was. It was a time when the conversation didn't stop flowing until we decided to call it night at 3am. There was a moment where I thought we might kiss, and we didn't but even without it, it was a wonderful night. Sometimes those nights are better.

I'm sneaking the book on her table when I hear the front door. I jump back into the hallway and quietly shut her door.

"It is SO cold out!" Morgan comes in stomping the snow off her boots.

"Did it snow again?" I ask, looking out the windows. The streets are starting to look like a winter wonderland again.

"Yes, it's just starting as I was coming in. I'm *freezing*," she says with her teeth chattering.

"Want a hot cocoa?" This is quickly becoming part of our nightly ritual.

"Actually, I think I'm going to take a shower. My foot needs to soak, the walk was good for it though," she assures me. I had offered to take Noel over but she insisted I take some time to relax for once.

"Okay." I smile. Retreating into my room, I wait until I hear the water running to pick up my book. It's distracting, knowing she's just a room away, but I try to focus on my book. Fifteen minutes later while on the same page, I hear the water stop and I wonder if she's noticed the book yet. I feel like a little kid waiting for my parents to tell me it's okay to wake up and check under the Christmas tree.

I realize that if I'm in my room, we'll never be able to talk about the book so I grab my book, a blanket, and find a comfy spot on the couch. I place my feet on the ottoman and think about grabbing a cup of hot coffee but I am already anxious enough. The last thing I need is more caffeine added to this situation. With my luck, Morgan won't want to do any reading tonight.

"Lucy! Did you leave me another book?!" Morgan comes rushing down the hall with the book in hand.

"I might have." I smile lightly.

"You're lucky I have something to give you tonight." Morgan smirks. She pulls another book from behind her back and it's a cover I actually recognize. *Meet Me Halfway* by Dee Lagasse, a book about a single mom who ends up falling in love with her boss. The premise isn't lost on me but I take it from her, pretending to read the back cover.

"This is for me to read?"

"I thought you might read one of my favorites while I read the ones you keep leaving me," she explains. Then she picks up one of the new holiday blankets, sits across from me on the couch, and takes a seat. She piles her wet hair in a messy bun on her head and I glance at her from over the book. I put down the one I was reading for a quick re-read of this one, just in case there is anything I am missing.

Everything is silent except for our light breathing and the sound of the pages turning. Every so often, I glance at her. Watching her expressions change as she reads. She must be a quick reader too because before long she's already halfway done with the book. I almost want to pick up my pace to catch up. She's smiling at the pages, the way a true book lover does. But it's when she extends her long legs under the blankets, we start playing footsie. At first it's innocent, her foot brushing against mine. But then she curves it along the outside of my upper thigh, and I know she is teasing me. Her face is unchanging as she extends her leg, then brings it back just as she reaches my hip. It's only when she puts the book down that she looks at me with a maniacal smirk. I'm more flustered than I want to admit but she does something to me.

"How's your book?" she asks innocently.

"G-Great, how's yours?" I stutter, falling over my own words.

"Riveting." She smirks. For half a second I wonder if she means the book. *Stirred* by Charity Ferrell is one of my favorites and definitely the definition of a slow burn. But I hadn't picked it for that, I chose it because of the forbidden relationship and the blurred lines that get buried. For the single dad who finds love in someone unexpected.

"I'd almost think you were trying to tell me something with these books." She smirks knowingly. I guess I had been more obvious than I thought.

"Oh yeah?" I try to play it cool, but all my nerves are rising to the surface.

"Lucy, if you want to fuck me again, all you have to do is ask," she says with a light shrug, biting her bottom lip. What I'd do to be that bottom lip but my own lips are as dry as a dessert. I can't bring myself to say anything.

"W-what?" I finally mumble.

"We can play the games if you want, but I think you want to be touched again. And I know exactly what you like." She slides forward, sitting cross-legged right in front of me.

"Morgan," I draw out her name.

"Luce." She's never called me that before but I like the way it sounds coming from her.

We are at a standstill, her just inches from me waiting for the go ahead for something more to happen. I am frozen, knowing if I give in to my desires everything will change. But my want for her outweighs my need to be responsible in this moment.

"So?" She's waiting, tilting her head to the side with a small smirk. That damn smirk.

"I want you," I say finally and she closes the distance between us.

Morgan's hands are in my hair, her lips crashing into mine like two drunk chicks at a party. She wants this as much as I do. I am soaked from her teasing, waiting for her to make a bigger move so when her hand falls between us to remove the blankets, I laugh as she throws them to the ground. Climbing on top of me, her lips find my neck. Kissing quickly like she can't get enough of me, her hands are pawing at my clothes, begging for them to come off.

"You are so sexy," she stops to whisper in my ear and I know I'm blushing. Never in my life have I felt so *wanted*.

Morgan slowly, achingly slowly unbuttons my shirt. Stopping to kiss each piece of skin that was newly exposed. Leaving me wishing I was wearing something sexier than one of my work bras. She doesn't seem to care because as soon as my shirt is off, my bra is on the floor too. Morgan stops to lick each breast, pebbling my nipples immediately with her cool tongue. She takes each one between her teeth just rough enough to leave me gasping for more.

"Please," I beg. I guess I'm not above that anymore.

"Please what?" She smirks, having way too much fun with this.

"Fuck me," I whimper.

"Okay, baby." She kisses my lips gently before sliding down the couch and untying my sweatpants with her teeth. With her fucking teeth. Something tells me I am out of my league but I don't care. I am going to enjoy every second of this.

"Should we move to your room?" Morgan asks as she slides my pants down one leg at a time.

"Why?" I ask confused.

"Because you're already soaked and I don't want to ruin this couch or be afraid for you to give me everything." Her confidence about making me cum is more of a turn on than I care to admit.

I pause for a second, only a second because she is trailing her fingers over my panty covered core and I am already dripping through. "Yes, bedroom." I nod and she takes my hand. We leave everything behind and it makes me a little more aware of how naked I am.

"God, you have the best ass." She groans walking behind me. I fall into my bed and she's climbing on top of me, resuming her position.

Morgan's lips meet mine and my hands are all over her still covered breasts. Which to my surprise she's not wearing a bra, just a thin t-shirt between me and her perfectly round breasts. Each one fitting in my hand like they were made for me. I tug her shirt over her head and I get a glimpse of how beautiful they are. It is like seeing everything again for the first time since last time we were in the darkness of her apartment. She is even sexier than I remembered.

THIRTEEN

Morgan

I don't know what came over me. *No,* I know exactly what did. *Lucy.* There is something riveting and intriguing about her. Something innately sexual and begging to be discovered about her. Ever since that kiss, I've been dying to get my hands on her. Then when she gave me that book, I knew she wanted the same thing. I'm going to play games with her any longer. I want her in my bed, begging me to touch her, screaming my name. Now I am halfway there.

Lucy is naked, except for the thinnest pair of panties that are already soaked through with her wetness. I am on top of her, trailing my fingers down her hips, grabbing her ass and kissing those delicate lips of hers.

"I- I want to be fucked." She whimpers again and I know she must be desperate for my touch but I am having too much fun teasing her.

"I'll be right back." I kiss her lightly and climb off her, running to my room as she calls after me. I don't want to stop once I get started and all I want is her touch. I work as quickly as I can, grabbing something from my nightstand

and then stumbling into the back of my closet to grab something else she is already familiar with.

"Where did you go?" She frowns and that's when I notice her panties are off and her hand is between her legs, touching her very wet core.

"Fuck, did you start without me?" I groan. She is so fucking sexy.

"Well, I didn't know if you were coming back." Lucy gives me these eyes that can only be described as a cross between a woodland creature and lust. I am putty as she looks at me but then her face lights up and I remind myself who's in charge.

"I guess you don't want me to use this on you then?" I hold up my strap on and her eyes widen.

"No, I want it." She sits up in bed, crawling over to me.

"Then I want you to wait for me. You can't start without me." I glare as best as I can.

"Okay, I'm sorry," she whispers and I lean in, like I'm about to kiss her only to brush some hair out of her face.

"Lay back down, now." I command. She fumbles back into the pillows and I decide not to put the strap on right away. Instead I put it down, holding onto my vibrator instead.

"I want to try something new, is that okay, baby?" I ask, climbing into the bed with her.

"Yes, please." She looks at me a little worried so I place a kiss on her forehead and she relaxes.

First, I duck between her legs, licking her sweet pussy. She tastes delicious and whimpers out with each deliberate touch. As much as I want to keep eating her out and watch her cum, I stop myself. I have plans for her tonight and I can't get distracted. So I lift one leg up, pushing it as far back as it can go. And for someone a bit older, she is incredibly flexible.

"Should I ask what we're attempting here?" she asks with a light laugh.

"Do you trust me?" I ask instead of answering.

"Yes," she says after a quick pause.

So I position myself with one leg over hers and the other under, with our cores basically touching when she gasps at the contact. She opens her mouth but instead I grab the vibrator, slide it between our legs and it hits our clits at the same time, causing us both to cry out.

"Fuck!" She moans and I lean into her, letting the vibrator hit. I begin rocking my hips back gently, following the sounds of Lucy's whimpers.

"Feel good, baby?" I smirk.

"So good." She closes her eyes and throws her head back into the pillows. She's touching her breasts, her hardened nipples and slides a hand down her stomach. I'm dying to touch her but between balancing, rocking my hips, and holding the vibrator in place it's hard to do much else. But goddamn, does it feel so fucking good.

I turn up the vibrator and her hips buck under mine. A gasp and light whimper rises from her lips and I know I'm playing with fire but I can't help myself. So I turn it up one last time and she almost jumps out of the bed from the sensation. It's only a few seconds later that she's breathing heavier and I can feel her orgasm building.

"Say my name when you cum." I smirk.

"Oh- fuck," she calls out as the orgasm hits her. I move my hips a few more times to really let it hit her.

"Oh, Morgan!" she calls and I can feel my own orgasm building. There is something sexy about someone else calling out your name. Just as Morgan's orgasms stops, I'm about to pull away when she reaches between us to hold the vibrator to my clit and watches as she pushes me over the edge.

"Fuck!" I scream, moaning as I fall back into the pillows.

"Mmm, that was hot." She smiles and curls up next to me. I take the vibrator, shutting it off and throwing it aside as we both catch our breath.

"You're so sexy, I've wanted to do that for far too long," I admit.

"Me too," She blushes and hides herself in my chest but I tilt her chin to look at me.

"Never be ashamed for wanting good sex." I pull her forward to kiss me.

In the morning, I wake in Lucy's bed with her lightly snoring next to me. Her mouth slightly agape as she sleeps peacefully curled up in my arms. I lost track of how many times we had sex last night but each time was better than the last. I don't know who fell asleep first, but it was some of the best sleep I've ever had. I'm not normally a sleep-over kind of gal but it seemed awkward to get up and go next door. Besides, it felt natural with Lucy to stay with her. She didn't expect it, which made it easier on me. There is nothing I hate more than someone clingy, begging me to stay over.

"Oh, good morning." Lucy wakes with a yawn and a small stretch.

"Good morning." I kiss her lightly on the lips. We both have morning breath but I didn't care. *What is going on with me lately?*

"I have something for you." She smiles.

"Oh, yeah? I hope it involves some of what we did last

night." I smirk.

She blushes and shoves me playfully. "It's on my dress-er." She points to the top where I can see a book but I can't make out the cover. I slide out of bed, strut over, and grab the book.

"Mmm," she whispers biting her bottom lip while staring at me.

I look at the book as I climb back into bed. *Gravity* by Sara Cate, I'd heard of her before. She is known for her sex club series but I have read those already. I*s this something new?*

"It's one of her older books," Lucy explains reading my face.

"And it's good?" I smile.

"It's dirty and well written, you'll see why I chose it for you." She smiles.

"So is this a thing? Should I expect a new book everyday?"

"Maybe." She pauses. "Is that okay?"

"Yes, more than." I smile. "But I want some variety too, maybe tomorrow you can give me a thriller? Some-thing to keep me on the edge of my seat."

"Wow, a woman who reads a variety of genres. I'm impressed." She leans in to kiss me slowly, drawing out my bottom lip with her teeth.

"You're playing a dangerous game there, baby," I groan as she pulls away.

"Maybe that's the point." She giggles. She fucking giggles and I'm blushing like an idiot because of what she does to me.

"What do you want to do today?" I ask her.

"Nothing." She laughs.

"Nothing?" I ask surprised.

"Well, what did you have in mind?"

"We could spend the day in that lovely oversized bathtub of yours and then maybe go out for some drinks or something?" I suggest.

"Like a date?" She bites her bottom lip again.

"Yes, like a date." I didn't intend to ask her out, fuck I've never asked anyone out. But as much as I hate to admit it, Lucy is different. Maybe she is someone I can actually see myself dating.

"I might be free," she teases.

"Oh I see." I climb on top of her, kissing down her neck. Nibbling on her ear until I hear her mumble a yes. We fall into each other, our hands connected as I make my way down her chest again.

We end up in the bathtub a few hours later. Both of us with a book in hand, loads of bubbles, and playing footsie from opposite ends of the tub. I'm more relaxed than I've ever been in my entire life.

"How do you not live in here?" I put the book down on the small table she conveniently has in here.

"I do sometimes, if work is extra stressful." She shrugs.

"I might just have to come in here sometimes." I smirk.

"That wouldn't be a bad thing to come home to," she jokes and then her face changes. I know what she's thinking about; Noel. He is the unspoken element of this that we have avoided talking about so far. I know what is racing through her mind, *what does this mean and what does this mean as far as being Noel's nanny?* I am thinking the same things.

"I like this book, but I don't know why you gave it to

me yet," I say, changing the subject quickly.

"What are you up to?"

"Like halfway through." I hold up the book.

"Hmm." She purses her lips. "I guess I could tell you."

"Please, right now it's just dirty which I love. But I'm confused…"

"It's about finding love in unexpected people. Maybe the last person you'd expect to fall for." She kicks her foot toward me, splashing some of the water, and my heart starts racing. I have never been the type for relationships, *but is this what I am missing? Lazy Saturday bath days where you have sex all night long and talk about books?* I have to admit, it sounds a lot better than I thought it would be.

We get out of the tub when we start to turn all raisiny. Lucy wraps me in one of her oversized fluffy towels and I head to my room to get dressed. She agreed to go out for drinks if we could go to the place we met. Which is where I was going to take her anyway, Puzzles is one of my favorite bars in the city.

I grab a crop top that shows off my chest with ripped jeans and a cropped jacket. I might end up cold but at least I'll look cute. Paired with my black ankle boots, I'll have to be careful walking through the snow tonight. Fuck, I had forgotten how cold it was when I left yesterday. I can't imagine it has gotten any warmer. But a plan is a plan, and my girl deserves to be taken out on a real date.

"Wow." I audibly gasp when I see Lucy. She's wearing a blue dress that shows off all of her curves and makes me want to take her back to bed right now.

"Really?" She blushes and tugs at the hem.

"You look phenomenal." I pull her body against mine and drag her lips to mine for a kiss. "Everyone is going to be jealous that you're on my arm instead of theirs." I smirk.

FOURTEEN

Lucy

_____

"Wow, someone must have had a good weekend," Dylan says as she hands me an iced coffee.

"I did, I really did." I smile, taking a small sip. I don't even care I barely got sleep this weekend, I am riding high off the multiple orgasms.

"Was it the nanny?" Dylan whispers, coming into my office and shutting the door behind her.

"Yes." I nod. I don't want to hide it from her, I want to scream about it from my office windows. That's how good it was.

"Wow, I haven't seen you smile like this." She hesitates. "Well, ever."

"I'm just happy, let's not overthink it." I wave her away.

"I'm glad, you deserve a good fucking every now and again." She laughs and heads out the door.

I'm working on the proposal for my author's next two novels but I'm having trouble focusing. My mind is on last night and how much fun I had with Morgan. Noel came home late last night from his dad's house and I think he was surprised to find me in such a good mood. I'm usually such a wreck when Noel goes to his dad's. I know he's probably fine there, I just let my anxiety get the best of me so it was nice to have a weekend where I wasn't so stressed out.

Morgan and I still haven't talked about what we are and what it all means, which should stress me out but is surprisingly okay with me. Sure, it is driving me a little nuts but I was also wracking my brain when there was less going on between us. For now I know, I just need to let things happen and see where they go. Which I've never done before. I'd be lying if I said it wasn't scaring me, especially considering the Noel factor of it all. But there is something about Morgan that makes me want to take this leap.

"Meeting in five." Dylan knocks on my door on her way down the hall. It is our weekly meeting with Tony to keep him up to date on what books are coming out next season. I hate any meeting that can be put in an email but he insists on it every week.

"All right, let's get started." Tony claps his hands together, standing at one end of the conference table. I think he makes a point to stand because he is so much shorter than everyone else.

"We have six books coming out next term. Mostly romance with our two psychological thrillers," Dylan starts. She'd always been better at presenting than I am. I like being more behind the scenes of everything.

"Lucy? Are you with us?" Everyone turns to look at me and I nod. Clenching my jaw, I hadn't even been zoning out or anything.

"Yes, just listening to Dylan talk about next year's projections." I force a smile. I am so tired of his passive aggressiveness.

"Great," he drawls and shoots me a look like I'm a student in trouble with the teacher.

The conversation changes to the projected incomes for each book, which is the job of the financial team so I don't need to pay attention as much. I find myself doodling on my papers, which probably isn't a good thing if Tony comes around but he rarely leaves his side of the room.

They continue and this time I make a greater effort to look like I'm paying attention. In reality my mind is on Noel and Morgan. I wonder if I'll get home tonight with enough time to spend with both of them or I'll have a mountain of paperwork again. I am so tired of having so much to do when I get home, but I know I need to do it. *I mean, who else will?*

MORGAN

"I'm sorry, you what?!" Bella shrieks over the phone. Even though the phone she can deafen me. I am standing a block away from Noel's school waiting for him to get out. I don't need any of the other parents overhearing this conversation though.

"I slept with her," I admit.

"But she's your *boss*."

"I know." I sigh. This is why I called Bella and not Ellie. Who would probably congratulate me for '*getting that pussy*' and then high five me.

"What does it even mean? Are you guys dating now? Tell me you at least had a discussion about it." She sighs.

"We, uh, did not." I wince.

"Morgan!" she yells again.

"I know, I know. That's why I'm calling. I don't know what to do. I don't know what it means." I frown.

"Why are you asking me? You need to talk to her."

"It's probably not a big deal, I'm making it more than it is, right?"

"She's your boss, you need to find out where you stand before you lose your job and you know, the place you're currently living." She has a good point. I am at risk of losing everything if this ended badly. And it isn't like I have the best track record with relationships.

"I know, it just kind of happened." I sigh.

"You like her, don't you?" she says after a minute.

"I do," I admit.

"Then tell her that and talk to her. You aren't doing any good talking to me about it," Bella says, and I agree.

Glancing at my watch, I realize it's almost time to Noel so I quickly hang up and walk down the block, dodging nannies and strollers to get to his classroom's exit. I only wait two minutes before he's let out and runs toward me happily. He's talking a mile a minute about his day and how it's only a few weeks until Christmas.

"My dad used to do it, but can you take me to get something for my mom?" he asks, smiling at me hopefully.

"Of course." I smile. *Who could say no to that face?* "Where do you want to go?"

"I don't know. I want to get something she'll really like."

"I'm sure she'll love anything that comes from you," I reassure him.

"But I want it to be something *really* nice," he says again, and I nod.

"Why don't we stop at the park on the way home?"

"Which park?" He looks confused.

"Bryant Park has the Christmas shops. We can go there now and see if there's anything that catches your eye," I suggest. I usually go with Ellie and Bella every year just to pick up a thing or two for my family.

"I've never been there." He purses his lips and he looks just like Lucy. It's kind of adorable how much those two look alike sometimes. "It won't hurt to try, come on." I lead the way toward the park and he follows suit. Lucy has given me a credit card for emergencies or any expenses that came up along the way but it feels wrong using her own credit card for her Christmas gift. Hopefully Noel won't pick anything too extravagant.

We walk along the snow lined streets, the sidewalk snow finally melting into the streets. The park is a little more crowded than I expect it to be. Lots of families making their way toward the ice skating rink, couples holding hands through mittens, and kids being chased by their parents. Noel and I zig zag through the green tents, looking for something that catches our eye.

"Can we stop for cocoa?" he asks, sounding just like his mother.

"Of course." I smile. We order the kind with the huge marshmallow on top after I double check there's no peanuts in it. You'd be surprised by the things that end up with cross contamination.

"What does your mom like?" I ask Noel as we stop to sit and sip our drinks.

"Nutcrackers, ornaments, and snow. Oh, and hot cocoa. She loves that. She'll be so jealous she didn't get to try this one." He giggles. As he drinks he ends up with a hot cocoa mustache.

"Here, you got a cocoa mustache, mister." I hand him a napkin and he laughs wiping it off.

"What do you like?" Noel asks and I pause. I can't exactly say '*your mom*'.

"Dogs, books, and bookstores. I'm really into reading."

"I LOVE DOGS!" he exclaims. "I want one for Christmas but Mom keeps saying no."

"Well, they're a big responsibility." I hate how grown up I probably sound.

"Yeah, that's what my mom says. But I can be responsible. They're just so cute." He makes a puppy dog face and I chuckle. I would have a hard time saying no to anything he wanted.

"They are," I agree.

"Can we look over there?" He points to a booth that has Christmas ornaments and a variety of holiday knick knacks.

"Sure." I nod. He dumps his empty cup in the garbage while I hold onto mine. I can't down hot cocoa like I used to. I'm not seven anymore.

There's a ton of ornaments that catch my eye but this is Noel's thing. I don't want to sway him in any way, plus he probably knows his mother better than I do. I paw through the Christmas cards, some of which are too dirty for Noel to read but make me chuckle. He's deep in thought looking at the nutcrackers when he calls me over.

"Which do you think she'll like better?" He surprises me by holding up two ornaments that say mom in fancy writing. One is definitely more Lucy than the other, but I know he wants to do this himself.

"Which do you think?" I ask back.

"I think this one, but I didn't want to get it wrong." He frowns.

"That's what I would pick too," I say with a wink. He chooses the prettier one that fits more of Lucy's holiday decorations aesthetic than the other.

"Can we get it?" he asks excitedly.

"Of course." I smile. We walk over to the counter where the woman wraps it in a small bag for us. We both agree it's probably safer in my purse than his backpack so I quickly tuck it in the inside pocket.

"Are we going home now?" Noel asks.

"I wanted to look in one more place first." I walk him

toward the Strand pop up bookshop and smile at all the books.

There are all the recent releases on display, a lot of which I had already read. Then there are socks, bookmarks and other book related merchandise. The Strand is one of my favorite bookstores in the city so I always love seeing the pop up versions around the city. Noel walks over to the display case of older books and is careful not to touch it. I pick up a book from the recent releases and decide to grab a copy for Lucy. She isn't the only one who picks out books with secret messages.

FIFTEEN

Lucy

I get home from work earlier than I anticipated so I'm surprised when I find the house empty with no note. *Did Noel and Morgan not get home from school yet?* I silently start to worry since school was let out almost two hours ago. They always are home within fifteen minutes according to Morgan's text everyday. Speaking of which, I haven't heard from her all day long. I didn't think much of it until now. I pull out my phone and instead of drafting a text, I call her. On the third ring I start to panic and worry about where they both are. *Did something happen to them?* Surely Morgan would've said something if they went somewhere after school. I race to my office to double check Noel's schedule. He didn't have any activities today. *So where the hell were they?*

I'm about to call the police when I hear the front door opening. I run over and unlock it before they have the chance. Noel and Morgan are happily talking about something but I'm overcome with emotion as I pull Noel into a hug and breath a sigh of relief.

"Mom? What's going on?" Noel shrugs out of my hug and looks at me confused but I'm too emotional to speak.

"Lucy? Are you okay?" I didn't even realize I was crying until I stand up. My face is wet and they're both looking at me like I'm nuts.

"I didn't know where you were," I say to both of them. It's mostly directed at Noel, but I don't like admitting that I was worried about Morgan too.

"Oh my gosh! I'm SO sorry. I didn't text you, did I?" Morgan pulls out her phone at the realization.

"No." I wipe my eyes, and Noel hugs me again.

"I'm sorry, Mama." He looks worried about me, but I don't blame him. It is rare I cry.

"I'm so sorry, we stopped somewhere after school and got caught up with the time."

"Where did you go?" I'm not angry but more anxious about where they had been all this time.

"We, uh, stopped for hot cocoa in Bryant Park," Morgan says.

"Oh, and you didn't bring me any?" I tease.

"I told you she'd say that!" Noel exclaims.

"Why don't you go get cleaned up for dinner," I tell Noel, who nods.

"I'm so sorry, Luce, I didn't think. I'm so sorry." Morgan lowers her voice.

"I'm not angry, I was just concerned. I like to know where you take my son." I don't mean to sound so professional but I need to in this moment. I am her employer, her boss, and she is my employee despite what might be going on between us.

"I completely understand, it won't happen again." Morgan sighs. Then she glances behind me and reaches for my hand. She must have been checking for Noel. I lean into her for a second, taking in the comfort and she kisses my forehead.

"Thank you," I whisper.

"Mama!" Noel calls me and we jump apart as if we don't want to get caught. At least we are on the same page about Noel not seeing whatever was going on between us. Besides that one little mistletoe kiss, Noel doesn't need to know anything is going on between us.

Morgan heads to the kitchen after shrugging off her coat and I go find Noel who's in his room standing on his bed trying to reach something on the shelf above his bed.

"Can you help?" he asks with a crooked smile.

"Yes, what are you trying to get?" I ask confused.

"My memory bank, I have something to add to it," he says, pointing to the painted box that says the year. Each year we paint a new one and anything he wants to, he can add little mementos for the year. It has been awhile since he has asked me to get it down for him. I watch as he pulls out a paper from his pants and folds it small enough so it fits in the opening.

"What is it?" I ask curiously.

"Mama," he groans. We had promised he didn't have to tell me what he was putting in here if he didn't want to, as long as it was safe.

"Okay, okay." I raise my arms in defeat and place it back on the shelf.

"I'm making dinner, does anyone have any preferences?" Morgan calls from the kitchen.

"Why don't we go out for dinner? I'm in the mood for something quick," I suggest.

"Okay, fine by me." Morgan chuckles.

"Where can we go?" Noel asks looking at me.

"We could get burgers from that place you like?" I suggest.

"THE PLACE WITH THE MAC N CHEESE BURGERS? YES!" Noel doesn't wait for my answer, he's already down the hall, putting on his coat and boots.

"You guys have fun." Morgan smiles and I look at her confused.

"You're coming with us," I say, thinking it was obvious. "As long as you want to." I add.

"Oh, I'd love to." She smiles and we both grab our coats.

The place is close by so we decide to walk. Noel jumps in the snow the whole way and Morgan and I walk next to each other. Our hands both neatly tucked into the pockets of our jackets, not that I don't want to hold her hand. But it doesn't seem like she wants to hold mine since she quickly put on gloves the second we got outside.

Noel grabs us a booth as soon as we get to the restaurant, picking to sit on the side by himself. Leaving Morgan and I to awkwardly figure out who is sitting on which end of the booth. Morgan takes the inside and the waitress hands us our menus. Noel already knows what he wants so he's quickly coloring away on the pages the waitress gave him.

"Everything is good here, we've been coming here since I was pregnant with Noel." I explain. Those 2am cravings for hot wings were no joke but thankfully this place is open twenty-four/seven.

"Oh wow," Morgan says impressively.

"Anything catching your eye?" I glance at her and she's smirking at me in a way that make my panties wet. "On the menu?" I add.

"The buffalo chicken salad sounds delicious." She smiles, looking back at the menu.

"That's one of Mama's favorites," Noel joins in. I hadn't thought he was even paying attention but it just goes to show you shouldn't underestimate kids hearing abilities.

"It is." I nod.

"Then that's what I'll have." She closes her menu. "And a chocolate milkshake."

"Mmm, that sounds delicious."

"What are you having?" she asks just as the waitress comes back to take our orders. I let Noel and Morgan go first, deciding at the last minute for a crispy buffalo chicken wrap and waffle fries.

I slip out of my jacket, the restaurant warming me up. I place my napkin on my lap and wait for our food to arrive. They are always pretty quick here which is what I loved about it when I was nine months pregnant and incredibly hungry. My hand is on my lap until I feel finger-tips reaching for it. I look under the table confused, the hand feels too large to be Noel's but maybe he wants to? To my surprise, it is Morgan intertwining her fingers with mine. She's donned the gloves and gives me a small smile when Noel isn't looking. It is a small gesture that isn't lost on me.

She continues holding my hand until the food arrives. We're both starving so we dig into the food right away and the conversation lightens as we all stuff our faces. Morgan eats like she hasn't eaten in days but something about her devouring her food like no one's watching is hot as heck. I'm a bit more reserved but that might be the way I was brought up. I care too much about who might be looking and if it is ladylike or not.

"Mama?" Noel whispers halfway through the dinner.

"Yes?" I look at him confused.

"I have to use the bathroom." He glances at Morgan awkwardly but she pretends not to have heard him and continues drinking her milkshake.

"Okay, let's go." I jump up ready to take him. It is on the other side of the restaurant or I'd let him go by himself.

But after the day we already had, I don't want him out of my sight.

He goes in the men's room and I wait outside like a not so scary bouncer. He comes out a few minutes later with clean hands and we head back to the table.

"Oh, no, no he's not my son," Morgan's saying when we get back to the table.

"Oh, my bad. You looked like a cute family," the waitress says sheepishly and finishes clearing the table.

"What was that all about?" I look at Morgan, confused.

"She, um, thought Noel was mine. So I just said he's not," Morgan says with a shrug. I don't know why it stings when she says it. She's only speaking the truth but it is hard to be reminded of something like that.

We sit back down and Noel finishes his Mac n cheese burger that's like half the size of his head. Morgan starts picking at my waffle fries and I fall into an ease with them. I can't help but wonder how Noel would feel if I start actually dating Morgan. He seems to like her a lot but that is as his nanny. *Would he feel the same if she was my girlfriend? Would Morgan even want that?*

SIXTEEN

Morgan

By the time we make it home from dinner, Noel is jumpy from his dessert so I suggest he play some video games before bed. Lucy agrees and decides to join him. I still feel terrible about what happened earlier so I decide to give them some alone time. I head to my room and find another book on my nightstand, this time with a note attached to the front.

'Because you asked for something less romantic, this will keep you on the edge of your seat until the very end'- Luce

I change into some pajamas and climb into bed with the new book. *Lovesick* by Cynthia A. Rodriguez, the name sounds familiar but I'm impressed she managed to find another indie author I haven't read yet. I start reading and from the beginning I'm hooked on this Bonnie and Clyde retelling. Page by page, I'm intrigued by their story and terrified of how it might end. A few times I consider skipping to the end just to see if they get a happy ending but I don't. I need to find out for myself so I keep reading. No matter how much I want to skip ahead.

"Hey, Noel just wanted to say goodnight." Lucy stands in the doorway with Noel, both dressed in their pajamas. I had left my door open just in case they had needed anything.

"Sorry, I was reading. Is it bedtime already?" I check the clock on my nightstand and realize it's after eight thirty.

"For Noel, yes." Lucy chuckles. I stand to give Noel a quick hug and he heads to his room.

"I'm in love with this book. The writing is absolutely fantastic."

"She's one of my most underrated authors. I've been trying to sign her as a client," she explains.

"Well, you definitely should, her books would fly off the shelves." If they are as half as good as this one.

"Mama!" Noel calls, and Lucy excuses herself to tuck him in.

I climb back into bed and continue reading. It's past two am when I finally finish and I throw the book across the room. Almost immediately, Lucy comes running in with a crazy look on her face.

"Are you okay?" she whisper yells. My lamp is still on so I can see her dressed in her pajamas, hair in a messy blonde bun, and an eye mask on her forehead.

"Yes." I pause.

"I heard a loud noise, I was making sure you were okay," she explains.

"I threw a book," I whisper shyly. Now I feel like an idiot.

"You threw a book?" she asks.

"I threw a book," I repeat.

"Maybe I'm half asleep but can I ask why?"

"I was angry about how it ended."

"You were angry?" Lucy walks in and sits on the edge of my bed.

"The whole book I'm rooting for this thing to happen and then it just doesn't?! I was shocked and upset, so I threw the book. I'm sorry I woke you up," I add.

"It's okay." She smiles. "I'm glad you liked it."

"Who said I liked it?" I gasp.

"You did, I can tell."

"Fine, I did. But I'm still upset."

"It's okay, you're cute when you're upset." She smiles and I feel myself softening like butter. *What is it about her that makes me like this?*

"I have something for you." I remember that I never got a chance to give it to earlier with all the commotion and then going out to dinner.

"For me?" she asks confused.

I reach in my nightstand and blush, pushing my vibrator aside. Not that it hasn't been used on her. I pull out the book I grabbed at the Strand pop up today and hand it to her.

"*Just for Christmas* by M Leigh Morhaime?" She looks confused.

"It's a Christmas rom-com. I thought you might like it, it's something I like to re-read around the holidays to get me in the Christmas spirit," I explain with a smile.

"I'm sure I'll love it." She holds it to her chest and stands. "Thank you."

"Thank you." I motion toward the book on the ground. "Although I should've gotten you a book like that to make up for it."

"Hey, you asked for the opposite of a cheesy rom-com.

I believe I delivered." She has a point, I can't argue with that.

"Goodnight," I say with a whisper and click off my lamp.

"Goodnight." She closes the door behind her. I try to fall asleep but I can't until I pick up the book off the ground. Then I fall into a cozy slumber.

LUCY

I know I have to get up for work in a few hours but when a beautiful woman hands you a book, you have to start reading it. I turn on my lamp by my bed and put on my reading glasses. They aren't necessary most of the time but my eyes are tired so I figure I should use them. Diving in, it starts off as a cute story. Two people who are unlikely together start a relationship for the holidays. I can totally see where this is going but I don't put it down. There's something about giving books to Morgan and being able to talk to her about them that makes her and I, an *us*. It must be our love language or something because I swear we never run out of things to say when it came to books.

I don't know when I fall asleep, but at some point too soon, my alarm wakes me. The book is glued to my cheek with a puddle of drool I'm glad no one is here to see. I shut off my alarm, careful not to wake anyone else in the house, and let out a long stretch. I woke before everyone else, and I will be gone before Noel even wakes up. It isn't my favorite thing, getting up this early everyday, but this is what I have to do.

I take a shower, letting the hot water hit my skin. I'm careful not to close my eyes because I'm pretty sure I will fall asleep. I really shouldn't have stayed up so late but the book was too good to pass up and now I'm sporting a book hangover. I finish getting ready slower than usual, I swear I am dragging. I hope Dylan is getting the coffee today because on my way out the door I don't have time to grab my usual first cup.

"Damn, you look like shit." Dylan greets me with my iced coffee and I ignore her not so nice greeting.

"Thanks." I sip the sweet drink and close my eyes for a second.

"At least tell me you look so exhausted from a late night of hitting that hot nanny of yours, right?" Dylan smirks. It's similar to Morgan's but she doesn't exactly make my panties melt when she does it.

"No." I shake my head. "I was reading."

"Reading?" She makes a face like I've said something disgusting.

"Yes, Morgan gave me a book to read and I fell asleep reading," I say, shrugging like it's no big deal.

"I've never seen you sacrifice your sleep for anyone else before," Dylan points out.

"Your point?" I ask.

"Just that you seem to really like her, I hope you're protecting yourself in all this," she says.

"What do you mean?" I snap. Why would I need to protect myself?

"Just, isn't Vera set to come back at some point? Morgan is only temporary, I wouldn't want you getting hurt over someone that's set to leave in a few weeks." She frowns.

"That's not really any of your business." I clench my jaw. I haven't given much though to Morgan's end date recently. It is hard when she is here all the time, why would I purposely think about an ending date when it is just starting.

"Okay." Dylan opens her mouth to say something but instead closes it and turns to leave.

"Wait," I call after her. "I'm sorry. I'm cranky and I didn't really think about any of that. I guess I've been trying not to," I admit. But I know for Noel's sake at least, I should try to be more careful. He doesn't need to get anymore attached to her than he already is.

"I understand." Dylan nods and heads to her office.

I sigh and sink into my seat. This is why you don't stay up all night reading; as good as the book is, you'll regret it in the morning.

SEVENTEEN

Lucy

"You want to take me ice skating?" I look at Morgan, not hiding my surprise.

"Yes, why, is that crazy?"

"You do know I'm old, right?" I ask with an awkward laugh.

"First of all, you're not old. Second of all, you can skate at any age," she points out.

"I'm going to fall on my ass."

"And I'll be there to catch you. I thought it might be fun to do something together," she says, and I know what she means. We spend most of our time with Noel, not that she ever complains, but I'm sure she wants some alone time with me too. It is just hard with how much I work and how much Noel's dad has a tendency to flake on him.

"Okay," I agree.

"Really?" She looks excited.

"Yes, let's do it." I nod.

"Yay!" She leans in for a quick kiss. Noel is still home, waiting for his dad to come get him.

I glance at my watch, he is over an hour late and there

is still no text or call letting me know he is even running late. That's another thing I hate about my ex husband, his lack of consideration for others. He doesn't care if I have somewhere to be or something to do, he'll make me sit around and wait all day for him if it's what he wants. It's something that used to drive me nuts. I decide to duck into my office and give him a call. To no surprise he doesn't pick up but after the third attempt he finally calls me back.

"What?" he answers grumpily. *This is going to go over great.*

"You were supposed to be here an hour ago to pick up Noel, are you on your way?" I say calmly. I know better than to engage in his rage.

There's a long pause before he speaks.

"No."

"Excuse me?" Maybe I heard him incorrectly.

"No, I'm not on my way and I'm not coming. I thought it was tomorrow I was getting him and I'm not around today," he half explains.

"What do you mean? It's Friday, of course you're getting him." It's been his day for as long as we've been divorced. He can't play this game that he suddenly has no idea.

"Well, I can pick him up tomorrow morning but there's no way for me to get there tonight," he says nonchalantly. "Just have the nanny watch him or something if you're busy. I'll send you an extra check if you're going to bitch about it."

"Fine." I clench my fist and take a deep breath. I hang up before he can say anything further.

"What's going on?" Morgan sees how angry I look when I walk into the kitchen.

"I'm sorry. Noel's father is being a complete ass and he's not coming today so we can't go out and I know you wanted some alone time. But Noel has to come first and I'm so sorry." I ramble a bit but Morgan holds my shoulders and listens.

"Why don't we all go ice skating?" she asks without skipping a beat.

"Are you sure?"

"Yes. Noel shouldn't have to have a boring night because his dad didn't show up. Let's go have some fun, you both need it," she says smiling.

"You're some kind of perfect, you know." I'm about to kiss her when Noel walks in so instead I walk past her, making it look more awkward than I anticipated. But Noel doesn't notice or doesn't care if he does.

"When's Dad coming?" he asks, barely looking up from his Nintendo Switch.

"So he's actually got a work thing and he won't be here until the morning. I'm sorry, love." I bend down to his height and offer him a hug but he shrugs. Sadly he's used to this happening more often than not.

"BUT we're going ice skating!" Morgan exclaims excitedly.

"Right now?" Noel asks confused.

"Yup! Go grab your stuff." Morgan is apparently taking charge of our little adventure. Which might be even more of a turn on.

"Okay!" Noel's mood changes automatically.

"You too!" Morgan looks at me and moves her hands to say let's go.

I head into my room and change into a more comfortable and warmer outfit. Some thermal leggings, a thick oversized sweater, and my snow boots are much better for ice skating. Even though I know I'll be spending most of the time on my ass. Walking out, Noel's changed into something warmer but it's Morgan who catches my eye.

She's wearing a similar outfit with only different colored sweaters. We throw on our coats and head out the door.

Bryant Park isn't too far from the house so Morgan decides we can walk over and grab dinner after. It is great she is taking charge of our night, it lets me relax a little bit. It is a little crowded when we get there but Morgan buys our skates, insisting I put my wallet away, and we go to store our shoes. I kind of hate things where you have to wear someone else's shoes. Like bowling or ice skating, but I'm not going to let it ruin the night. Morgan had made such an effort, not only for me but for Noel too. I know not everyone would be so cool with bringing along a seven year old on a date. That isn't lost on me at all.

"Come on," Morgan waves me over and I stand slowly, holding onto the wall to put myself on the ice.

"Mama!" Noel calls and he skates like it's no big deal. He'd gone for lessons when he was younger and I guess it is one of those things like riding a bike.

"Damn," Morgan says impressed as I make my way over by holding onto the wall.

"Okay, I'm here," I say unsteadily.

"What about letting go of the wall?" Morgan gives me a look.

"You mean you want me to fall on my ass?" I look at her confused.

"No, I want you to try and skate with me." She laughs.

"What if I fall?" I whisper. Noel is skating close enough where we can see him but not that he can hear my fears.

"Let me catch you." Morgan smiles and I start to feel her confidence.

"Okay." I nod. I let go of the wall and Morgan steadies me with a hand on my lower back. I hold out both my arms so I don't fall and I feel my skates starting to glide slowly across the ice.

"See, it's not so bad," Morgan says and I try to nod, but it's enough that my body goes off balance and I slide backwards, falling on my ass. Just like I said I would.

"This is why old people shouldn't skate." I frown as Morgan helps me up.

"Stop calling yourself old," Morgan grumbles.

"Mom, you okay?" Noel skates over to make sure I'm all right. Bless his heart.

"Yeah, just a bit clumsy. Are you having fun?"

"Yes!" he exclaims.

"Why don't you two skate for a while then?" I suggest and Morgan frowns at me.

"Can we, Nanny Morgan?" *When had he started calling her that?*

"Sure." She smiles but gives me one last glance before going.

I help myself to a bench on the outside of the rink and sit by myself. It feels a little lonely but my ass is freezing from falling and I'm less at risk over here. I watch as Noel and Morgan skate around the rink, they're close to each other as Noel tries to be a little more risky than I'd like. He's attempting to do a circle with his skates when he falls. I'm about to race over to make sure he's okay but Morgan helps him back up and he's laughing a moment later. Damn, Noel handled that better than I did.

Sighing, I make another attempt to get on the ice. I hold on to the wall but this time I'm a little more brave with it. I wait for Morgan and Noel to make their rounds and they join me this time. They're both happy to see me on the ice and I know that's what matters. Morgan takes my hand and shows me how to glide slowly across the ice. She teaches me the basics and although I feel weird, like I'm sticking out my ass, it actually works.

She surprises me when Noel isn't looking with a slow

kiss. I almost fall backwards, getting so lost in it. But she's there, holding onto me and balancing me. It is like a metaphor for real life. She is the adventure I so often crave and lack, balancing out my conservative and safer side. Morgan continues teaching me to skate until our time is up and they call us out of the rink.

"Did you have fun?" I ask Noel.

"Oh yeah! We have to do that again sometime!" he says, smiling. I'm so relieved Morgan turned his night around.

"Maybe."

"Come on, you had fun once you got the hang of it," Morgan teases poking my shoulder gently.

"Where to now?" Noel asks, and Morgan gets a huge smile on her face.

"Hot cocoa!" she exclaims and Noel jumps up.

"Now that's something I can get behind." I smile.

We walk over to one of the green booths and Morgan makes me put away my wallet once again. Ordering us three hot cocoas with the biggest marshmallows I've ever seen, we look for a place to sit and enjoy them. There's a few small tables nearby, and Noel runs around chasing some of the pigeons.

"Did you have fun? For real," Morgan asks sipping her cocoa.

"I did, I like how good you are with him," I admit. I know she is his nanny but it seems to go beyond that. She really cares for him.

"He's a good kid, he's easy to have fun with." She smiles and looks at him. I notice the way she looks at him but I don't say anything. Instead I ignore the pinching feeling in my chest of what's to come when her contract expires.

EIGHTEEN

Morgan

Noel's dad picks him up first thing in the morning and I avoid him like the plague. Something about that man rubs me the wrong way and I'd appreciate not starting my mornings seeing him. I know he is Noel's dad so I am polite, and I wouldn't dare say that aloud to Lucy, but personally I don't see how they were even married. They are like two opposites but not in a good way. I guess that's why they didn't work out.

"You okay?" I rub Lucy's shoulders that are up to her ears.

"I'm just stressed." She sighs.

"About what?" I ask.

"Nothing, it's nothing." She pushes her papers together and I take a seat next to her at the kitchen counter. Grabbing her hand, I look at her.

"Talk to me."

"I have a work party tonight that I'm not looking forward to," she says with a frown.

"Oh." I straighten. *Did she not want me to go with her? Were we not at that point in whatever this was?*

"I don't want to go and I forgot about it until yesterday at work," she continues.

"Would it helped if I went with you?"

"You want to come with me?" She perks up.

"Is that not what people who are... whatever we are... do?" I tread lightly. I'm not necessarily trying to label us but I am wondering what she thinks about us.

"What are we?" Lucy asks and I know I walked into that one.

"I don't know," I admit honestly. "I just know I like you, a lot."

"You do?"

"I thought that was fairly obvious." I smile.

"I'm worried about what will happen when your contract is up," she says with a heavy sigh.

I hesitate. I don't want to promise something I don't know if I can keep.

"Why don't we worry about that when it gets here? For now, I know that I like you and I like being with you. Can that be enough?"

"And Noel?" she asks quietly.

"You and Noel are a package deal. One that I'm happy to take part of. I love him more than I thought I would," I admit.

She doesn't speak, but stands and presses her lips against mine. It's in a hungry, almost desirable way. I know what she's trying to tell me, but I want to hear her say it so I pull away.

"So? What are we?" I ask with a smirk.

"I'd like you to be mine, whatever that means. I just want you in my life, the way we've been doing things. We don't have to label it if you don't want to," she assures me. I breathe a little lighter. "I just want you." I kiss her, our lips crashing into each other.

After having sex on the kitchen counter, and then in my bed and in the shower, we are finally getting ready for Lucy's work party. I am actually excited for it. Lucy is wearing this beautiful green dress that only highlights her long blonde curls and bright blue eyes. She isn't wearing heels tonight, but I am so with my extra height, I tower over her. Luckily I have a dress I've only worn once or twice that is appropriate enough for a work event. It is red, just above the knee, and I pair it with some tights and my best jewelry. I want to look the part of the dedicated trophy girlfriend.

"Are you ready?" Lucy calls from her room.

"Yes!" I walk out and her jaw drops.

"Is your friend Bella going to be there again?" Lucy asks and I look at her confused.

"She was at the last party?"

"Oh, I thought you knew. Yeah, she seems to be with my friend Dylan," Lucy says with a casual shrug.

"Hmmm." I frown. *Why hadn't Bella said anything to Ellie and I?*

"I'm sorry, she is your friend, right?"

"She is, I just didn't know she was seeing anyone." Then I think about what Bella does for a living. It isn't my place to tell Lucy and possibly out Bella and Dylan. Paying for an escort is no one's business but theirs and despite it being Lucy, I can't do that to my best friend so I keep my mouth shut.

"Maybe it's new? Does she know about me?" she asks hesitantly.

"No," I admit. "But that's only because I didn't know what to tell her we were."

"That makes sense." She nods. "The car's outside."

We make our way to the limo, not a car, and I'm immediately impressed. Is this the kind of lifestyle Lucy always has when she is working? She slides in first and I close the door behind us. It only takes a few minutes to get there but she gives me a run down of her boss and Dylan. I am worried she might be embarrassed to be going with someone younger than her but if anything, she looks elated.

"Do I need to worry about saying anything stupid?" I'm not normally the worrying type but I am about to take a dip in her world. The last thing I want to do is mess it up.

"No, you just be yourself. Everyone will love you." She smiles and squeezes my hand lightly.

The driver opens our door when we get there and he helps me out. There's a bit more lights and paparazzi than I'm used to, but then again I know Lucy works with some high end clients. Not all the people she signs as authors are nameless, she often signs bigger celebrities who are dying to tell their stories. I help Lucy out of the limo and she holds on tightly to my hand. We hadn't really discussed it beforehand, but I am relieved to be on her arm.

"That wasn't so bad, was it?" Lucy whispers as we get inside, past all the flashing lights and cameras.

"Nothing's bad when I'm with you." I know as soon as I say it, it's the most cliche thing to come out of my mouth. But I can't help it, when I'm with her, this side just comes out naturally.

"How much did that pain you to say that?" she teases.

"So much." I wince.

"Come on, let's get you a drink." She leads me to the bar in the middle of the room. It is decorated like a holiday party, with white lights, fake snow, and snowflakes everywhere.

She orders us two vodka cranberries, and I smile that she remembers what I drank that first night together. Clinking our cups together, we both take a hearty sip. She points out some of the authors she knows and her boss across the room. He looks like a douchebag but I smile politely as she explains what an asshole he is. I have the urge to tell him off, but I know better than to mess with her career. Bella walks into the room with an older brunette I assume to be Dylan, and Bella's face drops when she sees me. I don't blame her, but I hope she wouldn't think I would blow her cover either.

"Dylan, this is Morgan. Morgan, this is my friend and co-worker, Dylan," Lucy introduces us.

"Hey, Bella." I smile.

"Hey, I didn't know you were coming tonight." She looks nervous.

"It was a last minute surprise, I didn't want to come alone," Lucy explains wrapping her arm around my waist. Suddenly it feels more awkward with Bella and the way she's looking at me.

"Why don't you introduce me to some people?" I suggest to Lucy who happily smiles.

"We'll catch up later." I smile at Bella and Dylan.

Lucy leads me to a group of newer authors she's in the process of signing so I turn on the charm. We talk about all the perks of working for Lucy and what a great person she is and it's definitely my area of expertise to talk. I could talk about Lucy all day long if someone let me. Lucy's hand finds my ass and I wonder if she's trying to turn me on because, if so, it's working. But then she slips a hand down my inner thigh and I'm sure she is. She excuses us from the people we are speaking to, and I take her hand as she leads me away from the party. I don't ask where we're going, it's clear she either got us a room or she's looking for someplace for us to do it. Either way, I'm down without her asking. Hell, I'd screw her right here if it meant I could taste her again. I am addicted to her and I don't care who knows it.

"You were perfect out there, I'm sure they'll be signed by the end of the night." Lucy pushes me against a wall and starts kissing my neck. There's no one in sight, everyone around the corner at the party, with the loud music and chattering of conversations I doubt anyone will be coming over.

"I want you," I whisper in her ear and she bites her bottom lip, telling me she wants me too.

"Here?" she asks, wide eyed.

"Wherever," I moan and she pulls me further down the hallway. I wonder how she knows her way around this building but I don't ask. At this moment I don't care about anything other than getting my hands on her.

She finds a closet clearly meant for cleaning supplies and lets us in. It's a little smaller than I like but it is secluded enough where no one will find us and I can make her scream my name. We don't waste any time, Lucy starts kissing me and our hands are all over each other. I tug at the hem of her dress and drop her panties to the ground. She kicks them to the side and I slip one hand between her thighs, searching for her pussy. She's soaked, my hand palming her pussy gently.

"Oh, just touch me," she begs. I smirk, her wish is my command.

I bury two fingers deep inside her; her body falls into mine. I pump slowly, following the sounds of her light gasps as I continue. Swiping my thumb gently across her clit, she collapses into my chest and starts kissing my neck.

"Oh, oh," she moans lightly against my collarbone.

"Touch me," I whisper. I am dying for some kind of release from her.

"Why the hell are you wearing tights?" She groans.

Fuck, well I hadn't planned for us to fuck tonight. She tries to tug them down but it stops me from touching her so she gets frustrated and a second later I hear a ripping sound. She tears my tights down my thighs and let me just tell you, it is the fucking hottest thing I've ever seen. She rips them off my legs and throws them across the room. Then surprises me by getting down on her knees and starts eating my pussy. I don't have a second to react before her tongue is on my clit and her hands are touching my slit, burying fingers deep inside me. I throw my head back on the wall, and close my eyes, giving in to how good it feels. My orgasm is building when the door's lock starts to jingle.

Lucy stands and we both look panicked, we hadn't thought of an escape route. I quickly fix my panties but hers are somewhere across the room so she wipes her mouth and we both hold hands. A man opens the door and is clearly taken aback at the sight of us in here.

"You two can't be in here," he grumbles.

"Sorry!" I grab Lucy's hand and go around him before he can say anything else. He calls after us with something in his hand that I'm pretty sure are Lucy's panties but we both keep running down the hall and back to the party.

"Oh my gosh." We're both laughing harder than we ever have. Lucy holding onto me as I almost fall over from it. That was equally hysterical and embarrassing but we had too much fun to care.

"Come here." I pull her in for a kiss and our lips collide. Laughing between soft kisses, our teeth clanking together. Somehow it is one of our best kisses we've ever shared.

NINETEEN

Lucy

"Are you seriously banging the nanny?" My ex husband, Kevin, scoffs. I almost drop the suitcase I'm holding on my foot.

"Excuse me?" I clench my jaw.

"The nanny? Clearly you're hitting that now that you're a switch hitter. Good for you." His words come out like some kind of backwards compliment. He clearly isn't thrilled that I am seeing anyone, let alone a woman.

"T-that's none of your business, Kevin." I cross my arms over my chest. I've never been the best at standing up to him.

"Just remember not to lose all your money to the hot nanny because once you get remarried, I don't have to pay you alimony anymore. A woman that young and hot is just a fling." He does his horribly gross belly laugh where his entire beer belly shakes along with him like Santa Claus.

"Mom! I can't find my school book!" Noel calls and my feet move before I can think of a response to Kevin. Noel's digging under his bed for his school book, when Morgan calls from the kitchen that she found it but they're moving around me in slow motion.

It feels like Kevin could see all my insecurities about Morgan. Am *I wearing them on my sleeves or does he just know me that well?* Either way, I hate that I let him get in my head like that. I know the age difference between us is obvious. And I know Morgan and I haven't exactly been discreet around Noel. It is hard to be when she is always around and how strongly I feel for her. Still, throwing the age difference in my face like that is exactly a Kevin move. He can't bear to see me be happy so of course he needs to throw a dig my way. I try to shake it off as Noel hugs me goodbye but it is hard to think about anything else.

It is what I have been thinking for weeks. Morgan isn't exactly the most mature woman there is, and she is our nanny after all. I'm not being smart about this at all. Even if I end things now, it will be a huge mess that I'll have to clean up.

"Are you okay?" Morgan places a hand on my shoulder and I snap out of it.

"I-Yes." I look at her and feel this sense of peace. It is like she is able to calm me without even knowing it. Just being in her presence seems to make me less anxious and stressed out.

"Noel will be fine with his dad, I know you worry but it's only for two nights," she reminds me. Even if she doesn't know what I am freaking out about, she is trying to reassure me as best as she can.

"Thank you." I press my lips to hers and fall into her arms. Her lips melting into mine as she holds me closer.

"Mmm, thank you," she says with a smile.

"We should get packed," I remind her. I don't want to get on the roads for the Cut house too late.

"Car's already packed, babe, why don't you grab your

last bag and I'll carry it down for you." She smiles proudly and I'm relived. *When had she even gone to the car? Who cares, it is done and we can get going earlier than expected.*

MORGAN

"Are you sure you don't mind driving?" Lucy asks again.

"I'm positive." I kiss her cheek for good measure to assure her. I haven't driven in a while but it isn't exactly something you forget. Growing up right outside the city, I had to know how to drive if I wanted to get anywhere.

"Okay, just because it can be a little far. It's like two hours north." She frowns.

"Just more time in the car with you." I smile. We don't get much alone time with Noel being around all the time so I am looking forward to the time that will be just us. His dad is set to bring him up in two days and then we'll celebrate Christmas morning together at her Connecticut home.

"How'd I get so lucky?" she asks aloud with a large smile.

"It must be that nice ass of yours," I joke and press my lips against hers. Sliding my hand down her back to grab her backside with a quick squeeze.

"Morgan!" she chastises me with a huge smile and I laugh. I know I am embarrassing her, but I can't help it. I love having my hands all over her and the being able to touch her without worrying about who sees is easily my favorite thing.

"Come on, Luce." I open the passenger side for her and wait as she slides into the car. I check both ways and head to claim my drivers seat in her very fancy and expensive car. Driving it on the ice and snow makes me a little bit nervous but I know I am a good enough driver to handle it.

I adjust the mirrors to my height and start the car. The backseat is packed with all the presents for Noel. I place my hand on Lucy's thigh and she wraps her fingers around mine. Taking a small breath, I pull out of the parking spot that is a little tighter than I like. Once I make it out, I feel a bit better about driving and press the radio which is only playing Christmas songs this time of year. I don't hate Christmas songs but they aren't exactly the kind of driving music I am looking for.

"You're not going to find much else on two days before Christmas," Lucy says with a chuckle.

"I was hoping for some of the classics to sing along to." I don't know a single song that is playing. It is starting to make me feel old.

"I thought it was just me because I'm old." Lucy laughs.

"You are so not old." I shake my head. This is a disagreement we have often.

"I am, and that's okay." She shrugs.

"Forty-one is barely old, it's just MILF age." I wink and she giggles.

"Oh you shush." She blushes.

"Finally!" I say and turn up the radio as it plays "Rockin' around the Christmas Tree", but not some modern, autotuned version.

I turn the music up and start to sing, serenading Lucy and she's laughing up a storm. "Come on, join in!" I prompt but she shakes her head.

"Everyone dancing merrily!" I belt out and Lucy is cracking up so hard she's holding her stomach.

"One of these you'll be joining in, Luce." I shoot her a look but we both know I'm as intimidating as a small squirrel.

A few songs later, another song comes on that I know

and I hear Lucy mumbling the words under her breath. I continue belting out the words, not caring that she can hear me or that other cars in gridlock traffic out of the city can probably hear me too. I roll down the window and wave at the old man who's giving me the finger.

"Merry Christmas, Scrooge!" I yell and continue singing on the top of my lungs.

"You're so bad!" Lucy gasps.

It takes a few more songs and a almost an hour in traffic but Lucy finally warms up and joins me in singing "My Only Wish (This Year)" Britney Spears. We're both singing so loud that we almost don't hear the GPS tell us about our turn and almost miss our exit.

"I've never had so much fun on a car ride," Lucy admits as she turns down the music.

"You've never had a car ride with me. Now just imagine a ride but I can belt any song, especially oldies." I tease.

"Oh gosh, now *that* I have to see." She smiles.

"You will." I promise her. I have never been so open and free in a relationship before but something about Lucy lets me put my guard down.

"After we stop at the house we have to go to the tree farm and pick out our tree," Lucy says.

"I'm sorry, our what?" I ask confused. Where I come from, trees are made of plastic and come out of a box.

"Didn't I tell you we get a real tree? It's Noel's favorite part of visiting the Cut house."

"Cut house?" I ask.

"OH, well when Noel was younger he couldn't say Connecticut house, so he called it the Cut house and it kind of stuck. I was hoping we could get the tree tonight so we can put it up tomorrow and then it'll be all ready for Noel," Lucy explains.

"That's adorable, and yeah it shouldn't be too late after we unload the car." I pause. "Where are we putting said tree?"

"On the roof, I can't believe you've never gotten a real tree."

"I didn't think you were a real tree kind of woman."

"I grew up having real trees, so it doesn't feel like Christmas without one." She sighs.

"Where did you grow up?" I ask, realizing I don't know so much about Lucy's life before Noel.

"Connecticut, not too far from here. I went to an all girl's Catholic school in the city," she explains.

"Wow, I cannot imagine that." My jaw almost drops.

"The Catholic school girl part?" Lucy asks with a smile.

"Yes."

"It isn't my favorite time. My parents weren't exactly thrilled when I told them I liked girls too, then they worried it was their fault for sending me there," she says with a laugh.

"Are you not close with your parents?" I ask.

"They both passed away not too long ago. They weren't in great health. But before that, yeah we had a strained relationship. But let's not talk about this now, okay?"

"Of course, sorry for bringing it up." I sigh.

"No, thank you. It's just a conversation for another time, right now I want to enjoy the pre Christmas festivities with you." She squeezes my hand gently as if to reassure me and I smile at her.

TWENTY

Morgan

We pull into the Cut house, and it's like something out of a Christmas movie. The house is covered in snow with Christmas lights tied tightly to the house, a literal white picket fence in the front and a tire swing hanging from the tree in the front yard. I am impressed to say the least.

"What do you think?" Lucy asks as I stand in the doorway waiting for her to unlock the front door.

"It's beautiful, why don't you live here all the time?" I chuckle.

"A lot of reasons, come in." She waves me forward and I realize I've been staring.

"Noel's stuff can go in here and your bag can go in the master bedroom down the hall," Lucy says, and I swear a blush creeps over her cheeks. I can't tell if it's from the cold or not.

"Okay." I nod. I had grabbed a little bit of everything so I drop off Noel's stuff first and then leave my bag in the room. It takes me a few minutes to realize this is her room. Which means she is asking me to spend the night with her.

Well, more than just the night. No wonder she was blushing.

"You don't mind me spending the night with you? I can stay in a guest room if you need." I ask as Lucy comes up behind me with her suitcase.

"Well, there actually isn't another room. But even if there was, I want you in here." She hesitates. "Is that okay?"

"Of course, I was just making sure. Because of Noel and everything," I explain. We've been pretty careful about keeping our distance when he is around.

"Well, he's at his dad's and when he's here he knows we don't have another room. Plus that couch is incredibly uncomfortable."

"Oh, of course." I nod convincingly.

"Plus, maybe I want you all to myself." Lucy pulls me into a kiss. Her cold nose bumps into mine but her lips are surprisingly warm as they collide with mine.

"Is that so?" I tug at her coat but she pulls back with a groan.

"We have to get the rest of the stuff, plus the tree farm is closing soon," Lucy explains.

"Okay, Luce." I kiss her chilly nose and head back outside to grab everything. I don't want my girl carrying everything by herself.

By the time we finish emptying the car I'm starving, so Lucy calls in some nearby sushi we can pick up right next door to the tree farm. I'm still wary about this tree farm business, like is it an actual farm with animals and such? But when we pull up it looks like a lot of already cut trees and I'm even more confused.

"Hi, what can we do for ya?" a man with a thick belly and a full white beard asks. If you did a quick look, I'd be sure as hell it was Santa Claus.

"We're looking for an Evergreen, about six foot," Lucy says confidentially. I feel like the time I went to the car dealership with my dad when I was sixteen. He knew exactly what to ask for and I was left standing there confused about what kind of car I'd be leaving with.

"Oh we happen to have just two of those left. It's your pick," He leads us over to two trees that look identical but Lucy takes a moment to look at them.

I watch as she touches both trees, looks at the stumps and then picks one. I can't tell you what the hell the difference is but she looks satisfied so I'm happy to help the man carry the tree to the car. Lucy hands him a wad of cash and he helps me tie it to the roof so it won't fall off while we're driving. Somehow this was a lot less complicated than I thought it would be. I am nervous about driving home with the tree but Lucy double checks to make sure it's secure and that's enough reassurance for me. She clearly knows what she is doing when it comes to this.

"Do we bring the tree in the house tonight?" I ask as we drive toward home with the sushi on her lap.

"No, we leave it in the garage overnight to make sure no creatures are living inside. Then we can bring it in."

"Oh, has that happened to you before?" I ask wide eyed.

"One time three chipmunks were living inside our tree and then they ran around the house asking for toaster waffles," she says.

"What?!" I ask giving her a weird face.

"I'm just joking with you! That's the plot of *Alvin and the Chipmunks*." Lucy laughs and I face palm my forehead.

"You're killing me." I deadpan.

"We're almost home, we can curl up in bed with our sushi and call it a night."

"Or start the night." I reach for her thigh and I feel her shiver at my cool touch.

"Mmm," she moans lightly, and I know the night is only starting.

LUCY

Morgan's in the bathroom changing into something she promises I'll love but I'm pretty sure if she's wearing anything I'll hate it. It had only been a few days without her touch and I am desperate for a fix. I have never been like this before. Sure sex with Kevin had been okay, good even, but I could go a while without it. It was never something I had thought about all the time and wanted, no needed.

"Come on, babe!" I call out to Morgan.

"Be patient!" she calls back and I sigh, slumping into the bed. I am wearing my very best lingerie, a purple panty and bralette set that is sure to turn her head.

"So?" Morgan leans against the doorframe wearing a pair of red fishnet tights and a thick, Santa-like jacket that covers most of her body. I am confused to say the least, I thought we were going to have sex. *Is this some kind of fantasy of hers?*

"Oh, it's, um, nice?" I say, more of a question. I am incredibly confused.

"What about now?" She smirks and opens her jacket to show a one piece red lingerie that makes my jaw drop. Complete with the red velvet and white cotton to match the Santa jacket, her fishnets are stockings connected with these clips I am dying to set free. Morgan is always beautiful but she looks so sexy I am turned on and I haven't even touched her yet. Her blonde hair cascades down her ample chest that's on full display begging to be touched. I am speechless.

"Get over here, now." I finally say and she drops the oversized coat to the ground, sauntering over to the bed.

"I wanted to give you your Christmas present a little early." She smirks. God damn, that smirk is going to be the death of me and my panties.

"Is that so?" I ask, biting my lip.

"Let me do that for you," Morgan whispers. I look at her confused but she climbs forward and bites my bottom lip gently pulling it out, and I move toward her desperate for more.

My hands reach for her velvet covered breasts, her nipples hardening through the thin fabric. I squeeze each one and pull her into the bed. This time, I climb on top, wanting to be in charge. She fights me for a second, the role of dominance hard to give up. But she ultimately gives in with a smirk. I straddle Morgan, letting her take off my bra and slowly take each breast in her mouth. I moan and throw my head back, forgetting that I am supposed to be in charge. I paw her hands away and slide my hand down her stomach, unbuttoning her bodysuit and lowering myself between her thighs.

I take the time to kiss her inner thighs, brushing just past her core. Then I lean up, kissing her cherry red lips that match her outfit. I run my fingers through her hair and stop to look at her. She opens her eyes and I smile, catching her golden eyes looking back at me. She is so fucking beautiful, sometimes it's hard to remember that she's all mine. Despite never fully saying the words, it is clear she is mine. Just as much as I am hers.

I slide back down to be face to face with her wet pussy. I stop to touch her slit, dragging two fingers around her clit before sliding them inside gently as she moans. I love seeing this side of her, letting everything go, her face unreadable with pleasure as she falls back into the pillows. She reaches forward to push my head down and I lick every inch of her pussy. Focusing on her clit and the two fingers inside her, I pump slowly as she tugs just hard enough on my hair to turn me on. I'm already dripping through my panties, but my focus is on her. Despite how badly I want to rub my thighs together.

"I'm close," she whispers out with a gasp. I don't stop what I'm doing, not picking up the pace but continuing as her breathing becomes labored and her legs start to shake.

"Oh fuck!" She screams and lets go of my hair. Her perfect twenty-five year old body falls back into the sheets, her costume half off, half on. Her lipstick is still intact so I wipe off my mouth and devour her lips.

"Mmm, you taste so good," I whisper against her.

"I can taste myself." She blushes. I don't think I've ever seen her blush, usually the mastermind behind causing me to turn bright red. It is a refreshing change.

"You're so beautiful," I say aloud, brushing her dark hair out of her eyes.

"Stop." She pushes me away playfully but I hold her hand instead. Intertwining our fingers together and lean in for another kiss. First on her lips, then a soft one on her forehead.

"You're so beautiful," I repeat. This time she doesn't protest but leans in to kiss me. She uses her thighs to flip me over and climbs on top of me.

"Now it's my turn," she whispers. Disappearing into her bag, she pulls out her strap on and a shiver runs through my spine.

"For me?" I whisper and she nods. It looks bigger than I remembered it but I'm sure it's the same.

"Come here." She slips it on and crawls back into the bed.

Holding up my legs onto her shoulders, I'm thankful for staying in shape all these years. I need it to be able to keep up with her. Sometimes, I worry that with our age difference, I can't keep up with her adventurous side. She slides the strap between my legs, trailing it up and down my panty covered core. She slips them off in one swoop and throws them across the room for us to find later.

"I'm so wet," I whisper and she smirks.

"I know, all for me." She pulls up her long dark hair into a pony tail and then reaches a hand between us. She slides her hand through my soaking slit and covers the strap with my wetness. With one motion, she slips inside me and my breath catches. Pushing me forward into her.

"You okay, baby?" she asks with a smirk.

"Mmm." I nod. It is bigger than I remember. But it feels too good to ask her to stop. She thrusts forward, bucking her hips into me, and I lay back on the bed. Going achingly slow, she continues to pump in and out of me, causing me to gasp in pleasure.

"You like that?" Morgan wiggles her eyebrow.

"So much!" I call out. She is teasing me and getting off on it, that I could be sure of. But goddamn, is she not the sexiest woman out there when she does it. Something about a woman taking charge of me, *Morgan* taking charge of me is sexy. I know I'll be cumming in moments if she keeps teasing me.

"Kiss me, baby," she commands and I lean forward to reach her lips. Desperate to meet her every command. She smiles, her lips collapsing into mine, but our smiles stopping us from kissing. I wonder if this is what it feels like to be falling in love with the right person.

TWENTY-ONE

Morgan

"What about the Christmas tree?" I ask as we finish decorating the house.

"That's Noel's favorite, we can put the lights up, but we'll save the rest for tomorrow." Lucy smiles. The Cut house has much better decorations than the apartment in the city, and I assume that is mostly due to room.

"Okay." I smile and put the final piece of fake snow up on the fireplace.

"We have some time before he gets here, do you want to spend some alone time?" Lucy asks pulling me in to her.

"Oh? You mean some *grown up* time?" I wink and she blushes.

"Maybe."

"We don't even have to lock the door," I tease.

"We could do it right here if you wanted to." She wiggles an eyebrow.

"Lucy Mars, are you suggesting we have sex on the living room floor?" I pretend to be surprised.

"Or against that wall." Lucy shrugs, tilting her chin toward the wall.

"Wow, someone's getting adventurous." I laugh.

"I just want you." I murmur against her lips and she stares at them with eyes full of lust.

Lucy closes the distance between us with a kiss. Her thin lips softening into mine. We fall backwards into the couch that's covered in wrapping paper, Christmas bows, and bags leftover from wrapping earlier. I'm about to push it all to the ground when I see something red and shiny that catches my eye. I don't know how she'll feel about it but I am about to take a big risk.

"Do you trust me?" I break our kiss to ask Lucy.

"Of course…" she says warily.

I grab the satin red ribbon from behind her and hold it up with a wiggle of my brow.

"You want to…?" She looks confused.

"I want to tie you up. If that's okay," I add for good measure.

"I've never done that before," Lucy admits shyly, looking away. I tilt her chin toward me and smile.

"We don't have to do anything you don't want to," I reassure her. Placing the ribbon down I go back to kissing her gently.

"Can we try? I might not like it, but I'd want to try… with you," she whispers from under me. Her soft eyes searching mine. I can tell her curiosity is eating away at her.

"We can have a safe word." I sit up to give us a chance to discuss it. We've never needed one before this and I want to be sure she is comfortable. I know how big of a step it is to trust someone enough to let them tie you up. It isn't something I suggested lightly.

"Gingerbread," Lucy says and I nod.

"So you say Gingerbread if you need or want me to

stop. I just want to make you feel good." I brush my lips against her neck and she falls back into my touch.

"I want that too," she whispers, and I pick up the ribbon with a mischievous look.

I unravel it slowly, feeling the cool satin along my fingers and watching as Lucy bites her lip under me. I lay the ribbon across her chest, still covered with too much clothing. I peel her t-shirt off, smiling when I realize she isn't wearing a bra. I stop to show my appreciation for her breasts, taking each one in my mouth lightly.

"Mmm." She groans under my touch.

I tug off my shirt, leaving on my sports bra and she immediately goes to touch me but I stop her. I pick up the red ribbon and lace it around one of her wrists. I stop to make sure it's tight enough where she can't break free but not too tight where it hurts in a bad way. I lean down to kiss her and pin her hands above her head. Getting them together, I clasp them together and wrap the ribbon around her second wrist.

"That okay?" I ask and she tries to break free but can't.

"Yes." She nods. She starts wiggling her hips and I can tell not being able to touch me is killing her. She wanted immediate release, but I was going to have some fun with her first.

I slide my bra off, stopping to touch each breast while keeping eye contact with Lucy. She is biting her bottom lip and bucking her hips into mine but I am not giving in that easily. I tug down her pajama pants, only to find a sexy pair of red lace panties underneath.

"Someone had this planned, huh?" I smirk. I love that she wants to fuck me. It drives me mad how much she is into sex. Sometimes it is like rediscovering sex with her. Like I am experiencing everything for the first time with her.

She doesn't answer but I can see she's already dripping for me so I decide to tease her some more. Getting on my knees, I'm face to face with her pussy and I lick her slowly through the thin lace. Her hips buck and I can see her clenching her hands together. It must be killing her not to be able to touch me but I am secretly getting off on it. There is something hot about being in control, especially with Lucy. She is technically my boss but I love being the one in charge when it comes to us.

"Want me to stop?" I ask with a smirk, knowing the answer already.

"No!" She whimpers and it's music to my ears.

"Are you sure?" I push her panties to the side with one finger and drag it achingly slow up her slit. I stop to lick my finger clean when I'm done, watching as Lucy writhes in lust.

"Please," she begs and it's enough for me to tear her panties to shreds.

"Oops." I smirk and she's breathless under my touch.

I dive into her core, licking her clit slowly and running my fingers through her slit. I don't hesitate to put in two fingers, watching as she gasps out in pleasure. I pump them in and out slowly, reaching with my free hand for her breasts. She's begging for me to go faster, harder, to be touched all over. Her hands clasped together like she's praying and I wonder how good she'd look kneeling on the floor. But I'd save that for later, right now I want her begging. So I stop completely and she gasps out in frustration.

"Fuck!" She groans angrily. Trying to move her hands to do it herself, I smirk that she was tied up nicely. We'll have to do this more often.

"Tell me how bad you want me to touch you," I whisper.

"So, so fucking bad," she whimpers. "I'll do anything."

"Anything, you say?" I smirk.

She gulps but doesn't hesitate "Yes, anything. Just fuck me and don't stop."

I slide two fingers back inside her and she gasps at the touch. I pump faster than before, listening to her breathing and knowing how badly she wants to cum. I take a few licks at her clit and she's screaming my name, thrashing her head all around as she orgasms. Her legs are shaking but I don't let up until she screams our safe word.

"Gingerbread!" She squeals and I kiss her core softly.

I climb next to her on the couch and untie her wrists slowly. She's breathless as she collapses into the couch. I place soft kisses along her cheek. She is so beautiful all the time, but this is my favorite. Post orgasm when she does't care how she looks, she is stunning.

"Wow," Lucy whispers.

"So how was that?" I smirk.

"I apparently like being tied up," she says with a slight laugh.

"Mmm, I love the way you scream my name, baby." I press my lips to hers.

LUCY

"What do you mean you aren't driving him up?!" I scream into the phone. I know I should stay calm, but my ex husband just told me he wouldn't be bringing my son home for Christmas.

"It's too snowy and it's ridiculous I should have to drive that far." He scoffs. He knows I haven't had a valid license in years, it's not like one is needed in the city.

"We talked about this, you *promised* you'd drive him up if you could have him for Christmas Eve." I can feel the tears begging to pour out but I push them down. I won't give him that satisfaction.

"Oh, come on, don't start guilting me now. I said I'd *try*." He's lying and we both know it, but it isn't like I had any proof.

"Kevin, please. It's Christmas." I try to reason with him but I know it is pointless. Once he makes up his mind, he is as stubborn as can be.

"I have to go, this is my time with him after all," he says smugly. Half the time I can't get him to take him for the weekend but when it matters, truly matters to me, he makes a point to screw me over. It is no coincidence, this is the same weekend he made those comments about Morgan and I.

He hangs up before I can protest further and I throw my phone onto the couch in frustration. Looking out the snow covered windows, I begin to break down. I feel a familiar pair of arms behind me as I cry.

"Hey." Morgan turns me around to face her. She brushes my hair out of my face and wipes a tear away. "What's going on?"

"Kevin, he's not bringing Noel home for Christmas." I continue to sob into her. She wraps her arms around me but doesn't say anything. I appreciate her letting me feel this moment.

"I'm sorry, I just really wanted him home for Christmas Morning. It's his favorite day, and I'm going to miss it." I sigh. If Kevin and Noel had only known the huge surprise I had planned for tomorrow morning. Now I won't get a chance to give him anything until we are back in the city.

"I understand, can we go get him?"

"The snow, it's apparently too bad." I sigh. Plus it isn't like Morgan going to get Noel would be the best idea, I think that would only further fuel his rage.

"Okay, I mean it's only one day. We can celebrate when he comes home, right?" she says, but I pull away furrowing my brows together.

"What?"

"What?" she asks confused.

"How can you say that? Of course it's a big deal." I scoff.

"I know, but I mean we can make it special another day. It doesn't have to be tomorrow," she says, completely not understanding the point.

"Yes, it does." I frown and walk away from her.

"Why?" she asks, following me.

"Because it's *Christmas Morning.* I know you're not a parent but it's a special day watching your kid light up when they see the presents Santa left. It's the magic."

"What does that have to do with me not being a parent?"

"If you ever become a parent, you'll understand." I say but she scoffs this time. "What?"

"I know we're not exactly there yet, but I like to think of myself as more than the nanny at this point, Lucy. If I'm not someone who can see that magic, then what the heck am I?" she says angrily and I match her anger. Here's where her immaturity shows, no matter what, she'd always be younger than me.

"Morgan, it's just different." I sigh. I don't want to fight with her too.

"Right." She nods as if she gets it but I can tell this is going to be the biggest fight we've ever had. She walks down the hallway and I hear a door close behind her.

I sigh. All I wanted was Noel home for Christmas Morning, and maybe a girlfriend who is mature enough to understand that.

TWENTY-TWO

Morgan

"What are you doing here?" Noel's dad answers the door in his robe and slippers, which really isn't a sight I want to see.

"I'm here to take Noel to his mother's," I say with more confidence than I feel. I'd prepped myself the entire two hour drive but I'm still not confident enough.

"Do you know what time it is?" he says with a yawn.

"I know that it's late, but I also know it's his mother's day and she deserves to have him on Christmas Morning because that was the agreement you two made."

"Oh, she's one to talk about agreements." He scoffs, rolling his eyes.

"Just let me take him and we'll be out of your hair."

"The roads aren't good," he tries to say.

"I was just on them, I'm a very safe driver. We will be sure to text you when we make it to the Connecticut home." I smile for good measure.

"Kev? Who's at the door?" Along comes a thin, blonde woman that could almost be Lucy's younger twin. No wonder this guy is having such a hard time, he is still hung up on his ex wife.

"It's just the nanny." The way he says the last word leaves a bad taste in my mouth.

"Noel?" he calls out after a moment of our stare down.

"He's sleeping, Kev. What's going on?" the new wife says.

"He's going with the nanny. Lucy is threatening custody so I have to agree. Go wake him, please." He sighs. I notice that he still hasn't invited me inside.

She huffs and goes back the way she came. A few minutes later, a pajama dressed Noel is running down the hall into my arms.

"Nanny Morgan!" He smiles.

"Hey, Noel, let's get going."

"Hold on." Kevin leans in close to me. "This is the one and only time I'll be bullied into giving you my son."

"Have a *very* Merry Christmas." I wink for good measure. How the hell the Lucy was ever married to that man is beyond me.

"Are you taking me home?" Noel asks as we get into the car. I double check his seatbelt is done right.

"Yes, well, to the Connecticut Christmas house. You're a Christmas surprise for your mom." I smile.

I know I could've taken her with me, but I wasn't sure Kevin would actually give him to me, and Lucy didn't need anymore disappointment today. She and I had our first fight, which I fully intended to apologize for when we got back, but I thought an apology might go over better with Noel being there. I know I'm not a mom, but I understood wanting to be around your loved ones for the holidays. I miss my family and friends, but being with Lucy and Noel makes it all worth it.

Noel falls asleep the minute we hit the road but I keep

an eye on him anyway. The roads are icy, but bare. Not a single car on the road except for us which is comforting and terrifying at the same time. I'm glad I don't have to worry about any drunk Christmas Eve drivers, but if something were to happen to us, I don't want to think about how long it might take to get us some help. So I make sure to drive just under the speed limit, careful not to hit the ice the wrong way, and I sip the hot cocoa I made before I left. A little piece of Lucy I took with me, to keep me awake.

We pull into the driveway and I decide to carry Noel inside. He's sleeping soundly and the last thing I want to do is wake him again. I'm torn between stopping at Lucy's room with him first, but he's heavier than I anticipated, so I drop him in his room. Carefully taking off both boots, tuck him in and then knock on Lucy's door.

"Hello?" I hear her voice sniffle through the door.

"Luce, come out," I whisper.

"Why?" *Was she crying?*

"Please?" I ask again.

"What?" She opens the door and my questions are answered by the red rims around her eyes.

"I have a surprise for you." I hold out my hand and she looks down at it skeptically.

"You left," she points out.

"It'll make sense in a minute." I take her hand and lead her to Noel's room.

"Look, if you decorated or something that's nice but I don't want to see his empty room right now." She sighs. I ignore her and push the door open and her gasp is loud enough to wake the neighborhood but Noel only stirs.

"Noel!" she whispers at me, wide eyed. She runs in and kisses his forehead, tucks him in a little bit more and then closes the door behind her with a smile.

"But how?"

"I went and got him. Kevin wasn't too happy about that, but." I shrug.

"You did this for me?" Her eyes are full of tears and she holds my face in her hands.

"For *us*. I want the ones I love most around us." The words slips from my tongue before I can take them back and Lucy goes wide eyed.

"The ones you what?" she whispers.

"I love you, Luce, I'm sorry about our fight and maybe I don't get things the way you do. But I know I love you and Noel more than anything and you make me happier than I ever could have anticipated. So yes, I love you," I admit.

"I-I love you too." She smiles and her lips fall into mine. Our first 'I love you' is messy and unexpected, just like us.

Lucy lets me stay in her bed for the first time, and the sentiment isn't lost on me. Except neither of us thought through an escape plan for the morning. Which leaves us staring at each other half asleep when Noel comes pounding on Lucy's door.

"MOM! MOM! I'm here! It's Christmas! Come on!" You can hear him jumping up and down, he's so excited.

"I can hide out in here, until you go down the hall," I whisper.

"I think it's okay, we're both dressed. We're both adults," she whispers back. Lucy stands up, putting on her red robe over her nightshirt. I yawn and grab my flannel off the floor, tossing it on over my red t-shirt and Christmas pajama bottoms Lucy got me.

"Ready?" She looks over at me and holds out a hand.

"Yes." I smile. Something about this made us more real, but it isn't as terrifying as I thought it would be. It just feels *natural*.

"MOM!" Noel bangs again and Lucy opens the door. "Nanny Morgan! Come on!"

Noel doesn't hesitate before taking both of our hands and leading us down the hallway to the living room. The room is illuminated by the white snow and open windows, highlighting how beautiful all the decorations look. Noel drags us both out and Lucy sneaks into the kitchen while I take a seat on the couch.

"Mom's making coffee, but she always says I can start looking at the presents to see which are mine," Noel explains and I just nod, trying to take it all in. My family Christmases were a lot different, a lot more yelling and less *happy*.

"Here you are." Lucy hands me a mug of fresh coffee in a red and green patterned cup. I take a hearty sip and she takes a seat next to me with a matching mug.

"Okay, Noel, you start." Lucy nods and Noel rips open the first box.

"WOW! A new video game!" He holds up some game I've never heard of but Noel looks excited.

"Mom, you're next." Noel hands her a present. I guess they go in some kind of order, which is nice, my family kind of just opened everything at once in complete chaos.

"Thank you Noel." She opens a small bag that Noel and I picked out for her. Inside she carefully unwraps a small ornament that Noel picked for her. A snowflake that said Mom in red with a little heart for the O. "Oh, it's perfect." She smiles.

"Hang it on the tree!" he prompts.

"Are you sure? You usually like to put the first one."

"I know, but I want you too." I can tell this gesture to Lucy is a gift in itself.

She stands, and looks at the tall empty, tree looking for the perfect spot. Then she hangs it just right on the top layer and sits back down. Noel smiles happily and picks up another present. I had helped Lucy wrap most of Noel's and I knew what mine looked like so I'm confused by the unfamiliar wrapping paper.

"Nanny Morgan." Noel hands me the present.

"For me?" I ask confused.

"From me." Noel smiles proudly. I look to Lucy for some kind of hint but she looks just as in the dark about it as I do.

I open the wrapping and inside is a small, homemade book ornament. It's a stack of books hand painted by I assume Noel. It has the words Nanny Morgan written in his handwriting across the top. Feeling tears brimming in my eyes, I lean forward to pull Noel in for a hug.

"You made this for me?"

"I did." He smiles proudly.

"It's so nice, I love it." I smile, holding it up to show Lucy.

"It's beautiful," she gushes.

"It's family tradition to give ornaments, so I thought you'd need one this year," he explains, and the tears fall.

"It's perfect." I try to hold back how much it means to me coming from him.

"Put it on the tree," he instructs and I nod. I find a place for it close to where Lucy put hers on the tree.

"He thought of it himself." Lucy smiles and I wipe the tear away. I'm not normally a sappy person, but I know how big of a gesture this is coming from him.

"Can I open the rest of my presents now?" Noel asks excitedly.

"Of course." Lucy nods.

Noel begins tearing into everything under the tree while handing us presents every so often. We don't open them, waiting for him to open everything first, he's on rapid speed moving from one present to the next. Lucy definitely outdid herself, getting him everything on his Christmas list. Well, almost everything. Noel had been asking for a puppy for as long as I've been nannying for them but it didn't seem likely Lucy was going to get him one. I don't blame her, they are a lot of responsibility and work if you aren't home all the time.

"Thank you, Mom!" He hugs Lucy when he's done opening everything.

"Of course." She smiles and excuses herself.

"Want to play one of my games?" Noel asks excitedly.

"Sure." I nod. We're about to open one of the new games he got when Lucy comes back in and in runs a brown, gray and black dog in a Santa hat.

"Mom!" Noel drops the game into my lap and the dog runs right to him. Lucy's got the phone recording everything as she's smiling just as big as Noel is.

"Merry Christmas, Noel."

Scratch what I said before, Lucy got everything on Noel's list. She is definitely the coolest mother out there.

TWENTY-THREE

Lucy

I know I said he was too young to have a puppy and I swear I meant it at the time. But then I saw how much Noel wanted one and I couldn't say no to him. So I arranged for Rex, the dog, to be delivered Christmas morning when everyone was sleeping. I had to pray he wouldn't bark before then and no one would go in the kitchen. It took a lot of research but I got him from one of those last chance shelters up here and it made it feel like we were helping more than just getting a puppy. Rex was a little bit older but he was adorable and he was already well trained. His last owner had apparently died and that's how he ended up in the shelter to begin with.

"You just made his day." Morgan smiles, looking at Noel and Rex.

"What's his name? Is he a he? Do I get to name him?" Noel asks but it comes out as one extra long question.

"Yes, it's a boy and his name is Rex. I suppose you could rename him but he's had that name awhile and I think he answers to it." I purse my lips.

"I like Rex, it sounds like he's a tough dog." Noel starts rubbing his belly and Rex is on his back panting like crazy.

"I think he likes you, bud," Morgan says.

"Do you like dogs?" I ask Morgan. I hadn't even thought about asking if she was allergic or anything, I can't believe that. I mentally slap myself.

"I *LOVE* dogs," Morgan says proudly.

"Oh, good," I say, relieved.

"Does he know any tricks?" Noel asks hopefully.

"He does! Grab the treats off the kitchen counter."

Noel comes back with the huge container and Rex sits up immediately. I made sure to get the kind he really likes, something mixed with bacon. I open the container and hold up a hand to show him '*paw*' and he does it, shaking my hand so I give him a treat. Noel copies and when Rex does it, he gets another one. I show Noel all the things the shelter told me he can do like roll over, speak, jump, and play dead. Noel and I play with him for a while until Rex looks like he needs a nap. I got him a doggy bed and put it in the living room so he can hang out with us.

"What do we do now?" Noel asks. He is sitting inches away from Rex, waiting for him to wake up so he can play some more.

"We could watch a Christmas movie?" I suggest.

"Yes! Can we watch that one with the guy who falls off the roof?" Noel asks and Morgan looks like we're both insane.

"*The Santa Clause,*" I clarify.

"Yeah. That one." Noel nods.

"Sure, why don't we make some pancakes for breakfast first and then we can eat and watch the movie together." It is part of our Christmas tradition to have pancakes for breakfast together.

"Yes! Can mine have candy cane in it?" Noel asks excitedly.

"Only if you help crush them up." I wink at him.

"What can I do?" Morgan asks as we all go to the kitchen.

"You can change into your matching pjs because right now you're not matching the family," I point out.

"I don't have any-"

I cut her off. "There's a pair for you on our bed." I smile.

"Then I'll be right back." She heads down the hall and Noel hops up on the counter chair to help make breakfast.

I grab all the ingredients and a bowl and Noel starts mixing everything in. We've been cooking together since he was old enough to stand so I have no doubt he knows what he is doing. I grab some candy canes from the bowl on the coffee table and one of those meat mallets for him to break them up. You wouldn't think candy cane pancakes taste good but they actually taste a lot like Christmas, especially when you add just a bit of hot cocoa mix to the batter and drizzle Nutella on top. It is our secret family recipe.

"Am I allowed to help now?" Morgan comes out dressed in the red and black checkered pajamas, matching Noel and I with a forced smile on. But I can tell she is secretly loving it.

"Nope, you can watch. You're still a guest for this Christmas morning," I tease.

"Fine, but I'm stealing some candy canes," she grumbles and tries taking some pieces from Noel.

Noel finishes mixing the batter and I light up the stove. I let him do a lot of cooking but I don't trust my seven year old with an open flame by himself. I flip the pancakes as Morgan and Noel take it upon themselves to clean up and get the movie ready. Figuring out which streaming channel it is on. I miss the good old days of just putting in a dvd and being done with it.

"Pancakes are ready!" I call out one at a time and flip them onto Noel's plate. It's a trick I learned back in high school when I worked in a diner for a short time. I know he loves when I do that.

"Damn, that's impressive," Morgan says, watching on.

"I'm full of surprises." I wink at her.

We make our way to the living room, Noel settling on the small couch and Morgan taking a seat next to me. We share a candy cane decorated blanket and turn on the movie while we dig into our pancakes. I watch Morgan's reaction, waiting to see if she likes them or not. She takes a bite and smiles but then she makes a weird face and looks at the pancakes like she's checking them for something.

"Does this have peanuts?" Morgan asks with a scratchy voice.

"No." I wrack the ingredients in my head. Pancake mix, hot cocoa, candy canes and oh no. Nutella on top. "It has Nutella on top!"

"I need my epi pen!" she says, her eyes growing wide. She stands but she looks a little shaky on her feet so she sits back down.

"Where is it?" I call, halfway down the hall to our room.

"In my bag! T-the outside pocket!" she calls and I'm moving as quickly as I can, my hands shaking as I take each step. I find them and run back to the living room. She has a few hives on her face and she's holding her throat like it's hard for her to breathe.

I try not to panic as I remember the steps to do this. When she first told me about her allergy, I looked up some videos on how to do the epi pen. It was just in case something like this ever happened but I hoped I wouldn't have to do it.

"Mom! Is she gunna be okay?" Noel asks, crying, but I tune him out.

I mumble the steps to myself, pull down Morgan's pants to the side, telling Noel not to look and insert it in her thigh. I hold it steady as I count out the Mississippis in my head. Don't remove it too quickly or it could not work, that's what the internet said. Morgan gasps and I see her face clearing up right away.

"Thank you." She smiles, but I feel so terrible I can't look at her. Now that she's okay, I grab the three plates of pancakes and run to the kitchen, throwing them and the jar of Nutella in the garbage.

"I'm so sorry." I have tears streaming down my face but I don't care. I feel so terrible for being so foolish.

"No, it's a common mistake. It has hazelnuts, and sometimes contains peanuts. I should've said I don't eat any kind of nuts, not just peanuts." Morgan sips a glass of water and she looks okay again.

"Do we need to go to the hospital?" Noel asks.

"No, I'm okay now. They would just monitor me, and frankly I'd rather do that here. I know what to look for but I had such a small bite I'm sure I'm fine," she explains.

"Are you sure?"

"Luce, it's okay. It's not your fault. I'm sorry I scared you both, but it's okay. Truly." Morgan pulls Noel and I in for a hug and we both just hold her close for a moment.

Noel climbs next to Morgan and I wrap her in my arms. Both of us quiet as we go back to watching the movie. We don't move or speak, too much in shock from what almost happened just moments ago. I keep looking at Morgan, I'm not sure what I'm supposed to be on the lookout for but just in case the hives come back or something else looks off. Noel seems to be checking on her too, looking up at both of us every so often. I can tell he's just as nervous as I was from the whole event.

"So, I hate to be that person, but could we make a new breakfast? I'm kind of hungry," Morgan says halfway through the movie. Noel and I look nervously at each other.

"I can make it," she suggests and we both nod. I am going to be terrified to make her any other type of food for a while.

We head to the kitchen and she looks through the fridge for a moment and pulls out some cheese and grabs the loaf of bread off the counter. "How do grilled cheeses sound?" she asks with a smile.

"Delicious." Noel smiles.

"I'm not hungry," I say honestly. It's like the nerves ate away all my hunger.

"You should eat something." Morgan frowns so I nod, but I am sure I won't want more than a bite or two.

"Rex is awake!" Noel says excitedly and jumps to play with him again.

"So, I hope you won't mind, but can you go brush your teeth?" Morgan asks shyly.

"Oh my gosh! Is my breath bad? I'm so sorry." I cover up my mouth with one hand.

"No, no, but just in case there's any hazelnut leftover. I don't want to be afraid to kiss you," she explains and I nod.

"I'll be right back." I leave to brush my teeth. Scrubbing them twice for two minutes each just to be sure I get everything. The last thing I want to do is give us another scare like that. It is hard enough thinking about Morgan leaving in a few weeks, but I can't imagine her being gone.

TWENTY-FOUR

Morgan

"Can I go outside?" Noel asks, looking out the window at the falling snow.

"Uh." Lucy looks hesitant so I join in.

"I can take him!" I smile. I'm not the biggest fan of city snow because of how quickly it gets dirty but I don't mind this. The snow looks like something out of a Hallmark card today and I know Noel is dying to play in it.

"Are you sure?" Lucy looks surprised.

"I'm sure." I smile. I want to kiss her lips but I hesitate, we still haven't breached the PDA conversation around Noel.

"Thank you." She smiles and surprises me with a quick kiss.

"Ew." Noel scrunches his face and heads to his room to grab his snow pants.

"Sorry, it was just too long since I kissed you." Lucy blushes.

"I was thinking the same thing." I kiss her this time lightly.

Then I grab my puffy winter coat, my snow boots, and

throw on a second pair of pants and gloves. I put on my hat and I'm all set to go outside. I like the snow but I am not a fan of how freaking cold it has to be to get the snow. Noel comes running outside in his snow pants and jumps headfirst into the huge mountain of snow. I hear Lucy gasp from the screen door, but Noel stands up almost immediately with a face full of snow.

"That was awesome!" he cheers and runs back to the deck to do it again, his snow pants swishing with each step.

I pick up a handful of snow and as he's jumping, I toss it lightly at his back. He looks back at me, shocked that I would do such a thing.

"This means war!" he declares and I laugh, joining him in the pile of snow.

He takes one side of the backyard while I take the other and we both make a mountain of snowballs before starting to throw them at each other. I'm careful not to hit him too hard, the last thing you want is to be hit in the face, full force with a snowball. He's dodging them pretty good for his size, bouncing around on the snow like it's no big deal. I have to start building some kind of fortress out of the snow to keep myself protected. He doesn't have the best aim but every so often one or two of them hit me pretty hard and almost knocks me back on my ass. It's only when I run out of snowballs and he's coming over that I yell truce. But he takes a fist full of snow and throws it right at my chest. I make a theatric of it and lay back in the snow as if I've been shot and he's cracking up.

"Did I really hit you that hard?" He laughs, walking over.

"No." I shake my head and as he steps closer I pull him down by the leg and into the snow with me.

"Hey!" e exclaims and then starts laughing. He pushes out his arms and legs and starts making snow angels.

"Come on, you gotta make some too!" he insists and I shrug. I am already covered in snow to my underpants, *what is the difference now?*

I spread my arms and legs out and start moving them back and forth. It's surprisingly more fun than I remembered.

"Smile!" Lucy calls from the deck with her phone extended, presumably to take a photo of us.

"Mama!" Noel complains.

"I just wanted to capture the moment," she says with a smile and goes to head back in.

"You should join us!" I call out after her and she gives me a look that could kill.

"That's okay, you two have fun." She turns to go again but Noel calls out this time.

"Come on, Mama! It's fun!" He gives a face pushing out his bottom lip and I do the same so she'll join us.

"Fine. But I need to change." She sighs after a moment.

"Yay!" Noel and I high five and she mumbles something about thinking she only had one kid to worry about.

Lucy returns a few minutes later in snow pants similar to Noel's, a thick winter coat, and one of those parka hats that you'd wear if it was below freezing. She looks ridiculous and simultaneously adorable.

"All right, I'm out here." She gestures and Noel and I take the snowballs we were hiding behind our backs and throw them at her. She pretends to fall to her knees, clutching her chest similar to the way I did.

"Now you have to make snow angels to get back to life," Noel tells her, and I nod. Apparently that's what we were doing. I know better than to argue with a seven year old.

"All right, but I'm definitely going to need some help

up later." Lucy falls backward into the snow and begins making snow angels. Then Noel runs over and lightly jumps on her.

"Ahh!" She pretends to complain and I throw some snow their way.

"We need to team up!" Noel yells at Lucy.

"Against Morgan?" She looks confused.

"No! Against evil Nanny Morgan! Come on!" Noel takes her by the hand and tries to bring her across the yard to his snow fort but I've already got snowballs coming their way.

"You'll never make it there alive!" I yell out.

Lucy gets the brunt of the snowballs due to her size difference of her partner in crime. And if I didn't know any better I'd say that was part of Noel's plan all along. He seems to be using Lucy as a shield so he can make more snowballs or try to invade my fort. We play his game for a while until Lucy suggests we take a walk down the block and Noel can go sledding with some of the neighborhood kids.

The Cut house was on a cul de sac so there is one house that has a huge mountain of snow where apparently no kids live. Lucy says he used to have young kids but they are all grown up now so he likes to have the neighborhood kids use his yard. The snow will pile up pretty high based on the way the houses are built and it is the perfect size and shape for sledding. Noel jumps at the chance. He already has his sled out of the garage by the time Lucy finishes her sentence.

"Ready, Mama? Nanny Morgan?" I don't know when he started calling me that but I like the way it sounds. It is more endearing than my name and more than just the *nanny*.

"All set." Lucy is about to slip on the snow so I grab her

at the last second, catching her in almost a dipping position. I help her up and hold on to her gloved hand tight to
make sure she doesn't fall again.

"Thank you." She smiles.

We walk to the hill and there's a huge group of kids
about Noel's age. Noel takes off right away and Lucy and I
stand at the bottom of the hill near some of the other
parents.

"Want any hot cocoa?" one of the moms ask.

"Sure." I smile and she hands me a cup with a lid and
everything. I am impressed, *all this just to watch your kids sled
down a hill?*

"Which one's yours?" she asks me and I'm about to
correct her but instead I just smile and point to Noel. The
smile on Lucy's face is not lost on me.

"Mine's over there, she's a bit nervous this year." She
points to the girl playing in the snow rather than running
up the hill.

"Noel's a bit too fearless," Lucy says with a sigh.

We make small talk for a bit until the woman's
daughter decides she's ready to go home. We watch Noel
go down the hill probably a dozen times and then start
playing with the other neighborhood kids. I don't know if
they remember him from last year but if not this kid has no
problem making new friends.

"Do you ever think about having more kids?" I ask
Lucy. Whose jaw almost falls on the floor when I ask.

"Uh, why do you ask?" she stutters. *Damn, did I hit a
nerve or something?*

"I've just seen Noel with others and I didn't know if
you always planned on him being your only one," I say
with a shrug. I hadn't given it much of a thought before,
but I wouldn't mind having a few kids of my own.

"He wasn't going to be, no." She pauses. "I've thought

about having more but it never seemed right with Kevin. I kind of thought that time passed for me. But it would be nice to give Noel a sibling."

"Maybe one day." I look away, realizing what I've said. *Who am I turning into? I have gone from no relationships to the talk of having a baby with Lucy? She is changing me and I am embracing it.*

"Do I have to go to bed?" Noel complains as Lucy hands him his pajamas.

"Yes, we had a long day and tomorrow is another day. You need some sleep," Lucy says in her mom voice.

"Ugh, fine." He stomps his way to his room and closes the door behind him.

"I'll be in soon to read to you!" Lucy calls with a laugh.

"Seven going on seventeen, I swear," she whispers to me. Stepping into the living room, she looks at me and frowns. "Are you sure you're okay?"

"I keep telling you I am, Luce. I know it was scary but I promise if something else was wrong, I would tell you. We're out of the woods now, it's been more than twenty-four hours. I'm okay, I *promise*," I try to reassure her. She's been like this since the hazelnut incident of yesterday.

"Okay, are you coming to bed soon?" she whispers.

"As soon as you put Noel to bed," I say with a smile and she presses her lips to mine.

"Don't forget to check your nightstand," she says with a wink and I all but jump up to see what book she's left for me tonight.

Blurred Lines by Victoria Ellis, I read the back and it

sounds promising. It seems to be about past lovers getting together so I am confused about the meaning of this one. Maybe it will make more sense if I read it, so I pick it up and start reading. I only get about four chapters in when Lucy comes in and shuts the door behind her.

"Noel's already sleeping, he was arguing about it and fell asleep mid conversation," she says in a whisper.

"I don't blame him, today was a lot." All my muscles are sore as can be from the snowball fights and running around. I am not used to that much exercise outside of sex.

"Are you too tired for some kissing?" Lucy asks with a bite of her lip.

"Mmm, never too tired for that." I smirk and put my book aside.

Our lips collide as she climbs on top of me, my hands running through her long hair. Her hands finding themselves along my curves. I could kiss her all night long and never get tired of her lips. Something about them are so soft and addicting. I crave her touch more than I ever have anyone else's.

TWENTY-FIVE

Lucy

The last thing I want is for Morgan to quit. Not only for my sake, but for Noel's too. He's gotten so attached to her these last few weeks, I can't imagine the two of them being apart. I know I shouldn't even be thinking about this yet, I mean we still have another few weeks. But Vera emailed Kayla and I asking if she could be returning soon and I don't have an answer for her. Kayla is oblivious to what is going on between Morgan and I, and it isn't like I can tell Vera not to come back because I fell in love with her replacement. It all feels so cliche. I know Morgan's contract is ending but does that really mean she is leaving? Maybe she'll want to stay and I am worrying about it for nothing. Maybe if she knows she has the chance to stay she'll be happy. I write an email to Kayla asking her to draft a new open ended contract with Morgan.

"Mama?" Noel runs inside with Rex.

"Honey, the snow," I remind him.

"Sorry! Are you coming out?"

"No, I think I'm going to stay in where it's warm." I smile, holding my hot coffee. I had enough cold yesterday with Morgan and Noel. How they ever convinced me to make snow angels is beyond me.

"Okay!" He shrugs and heads back outside with Rex, who is dressed in a matching green coat.

Morgan and Noel are playing outside, I believe having another snowball fight from the looks of it. I am trying to let Noel soak in as much time as he can with her. Especially with everything so up in the air right now. I decide to make some cookies so we can decorate them later. I read the box three times, just to be sure there's no traces of any kind of nuts. While they're baking, I mix together powered sugar, butter, and a little milk to make the frosting. I divide it into a few cups and add food coloring to give options. They must smell the cookies because by the time they're out of the oven, Morgan and Noel are making their way inside with Rex.

"Clean off outside, please," I remind them and Noel picks up Rex, shaking some of the snow off him. Rex looks concerned but he's compliant in it.

"Mmm, cookies!" Noel smiles and dumps his boots next to the door. He throws his coat on the hook and towels off Rex so he's completely dry too.

"I thought we could decorate them." I smile.

"Only if I can lick the spoon!" Noel shouts.

"Aw, man!" Morgan pretends to complain.

"Don't worry, children, there's enough spoons for both of you." I laugh.

Morgan and Noel clean themselves up and wash their hands before taking seats at the kitchen table to start decorating. While they do, I make three cups of hot cocoa with extra marshmallows to warm them up.

I take a seat across from them, watching as they both put a lot of effort into making their cookies.I had cut them into Christmas shapes. They were originally supposed to be for Santa for Christmas Eve but when Noel didn't come home, I completely forgot about them.

"This is so much fun! Can we make cookies again soon?" Noel asks smiling.

"I don't see why not." Morgan smiles.

I don't say anything about how she only has two weeks left. *Ten days if you're counting, but who's counting?* I am.

The drive back to the city is the opposite of how it was driving to the Cut house. Morgan and Noel are in a good mood but all I can think about is how Morgan only has nine days left in the house. *What is going to happen when she leaves? When she goes back to college? Will we try and stay together?* I am too old to try and attempt a long distance relationship with a collage woman. Morgan must feel my stress because she squeezes my hand lightly, but I'm too anxious to squeeze back. It's like I know she's right next to me but I have to wonder how much she's in this.

"Are you okay?" she whispers just low enough for me to hear.

"Yeah," I lie and force a smile. It must not be convincing enough because she gives me a wary look.

Morgan's phone starts buzzing and she glances at it in the cup holder. "Can you check that for me?"

"Sure," I have never been nosy before but I am curious who is messaging her so many times. It seems to be some kind of group chat with her friends.

Ellie: Did you get the email?

Bella: Did you register for classes?

Ellie: WHERE R U

Bella: Are you with your GF? Did you tell her about the email?

I read the messages out loud and Morgan's face changes into a line. "Did you want me to say anything back?" My anger is getting the better of me.

"No, that's okay." She frowns.

"So, what email?" I ask after a minute.

"I got the TA position I applied for," she says slowly.

"Oh." I don't offer any more of a reaction. I guess it is clear where Morgan and I stand. She was looking for a new job without even considering Noel or I.

"What?" She looks at me confused.

"We can't talk about this right now," I snap. Noel may have his headphones on but I don't know how much he could hear. I am not going to fight with her in front of him, let alone about something that involves him.

We get back to the apartment in great time but once we get there, I lock myself in my office and tell Morgan and Noel I'm catching up on paperwork. It's understandable, with how many days I had off without touching a single piece of work. But in reality I want to go over the new contract Kayla sent me for Morgan. I want to make sure it is perfect before I show it to her. Plus I need just a bit of time to calm down from her admission in the car.

Now, more than ever, I need to make sure the contract

will be worthwhile for her. If I am in competition with an actual job offer from her college. *Is that something that she actually wants or just something she applied for to pay for classes?* I have so many questions I know I need to ask Morgan, but I can't bring myself to knock on her door. Not tonight. I don't want to know the answers. But I also can't spend the night alone after the day we both had.

It is reckless, with Noel down the hall, but I need to be in her arms. So I knock on her door, she's in bed reading one of the books I gave her with her hair in a messy bun. I smile, thinking this is how I want to remember her. She goes to speak but I shake my head. I climb in bed next to her and she opens her arms, letting me lay with her.

She's warm, wearing her thick flannel pajamas and covers us with three blankets. We don't speak but she lightly rubs my hair, twirling my curls with her fingers and I feel calm. It's like all my anxiety slips from my body with her touch. She kisses my forehead softly and goes back to reading her book. One hand staying on my hair, wrapped around my shoulders, there's only the sound of her pages turning and our low breaths. It's just enough to let me fall asleep without the heavy thoughts taking over.

TWENTY-SIX

Morgan

Ever since yesterday, it's starting to feel like I'm in the final countdown with Noel and Lucy. I don't want it to feel that way, but the way she's looking at me and the way she's talking makes it hard not to. I'm in bed and I finally finish *Blurred Lines*, which ended up being a metaphor for found families and unexpected families. The way Noel and Lucy have become my family over the last several weeks. I didn't expect to fall this hard for Lucy, let alone fall in love with being somewhat of a stepparent to her son. I know it is way different, but I can see us going down that road someday. Because it is easy to love Noel when I love Lucy so much. I'm back in my own bed tonight and it feels weird without Lucy there.

"Can I come in?" Lucy knocks on the door.

"Of course." I sit up in bed and she climbs in next to me.

"Can we talk?" she asks quietly and I nod.

"So, I talked to Kayla and she drafted up a contract for you to stay on as Noel's nanny for another few months until the end of the school year. And it's a little bit more money than now," she explains and I freeze. *Is she seriously offering to buy me?* It was different when I first took the job without knowing her. *Is she trying to get me to stay with her by using Noel?*

"Oh," is all I manage to say. It's like my head is spinning a million miles a minute. I don't know what to say without hurting her.

"What do you think?" she prompts with a smile. Is she serious? Does she really think that's what I want? I thought she understood how important it is for me to finish school.

"I-I can't," I say aloud and her face falls.

"Oh, I see." She clenches her jaw and I can tell she's angry.

"Luce." I reach for her hand but she pulls away.

"No, I get it." She stands and I reach after her.

"No, you don't. I don't think you do," I snap.

"What?" She looks surprised.

"I applied for that teaching assistant position before I started here. I had to apply for that months ago, but I just got accepted this weekend. I didn't tell you because I wasn't sure what I was doing yet," I explain. I hadn't even had a chance to think about it, let alone discuss it with her.

"Does that mean you aren't taking it?" She perks up.

"No, I am," I decide in the moment. It is what I need to do if Lucy and I have any chance of being together long term, I can't be locked into a contract with her as my boss any longer.

"So you're just leaving Noel and I behind? Was everyone right? Was I just some kind of fling to you?" She starts crying and I reach for her again, but she turns away from me.

"Luce, you're not a fling. You could never be a fling." I pull her into my arms and hug her tightly. She leans into my chest, sobbing lightly.

"Then what is this? What is this going to be when you leave?" she asks.

"I don't know," I say honestly.

"I love you," she whispers.

"I love you too." I smile. "I just don't want to stay because of a contract. I want to stay because I want to."

"But you don't want to?" She sighs.

"No. I need to finish school first."

"First?" she asks, confused.

"Yes, I need to get my degree and finish school *first*, then maybe we can talk about living together."

"Does that mean you're moving out?"

"Yes." I hadn't meant it that way, but as she said it, it sounded like the best option.

"But you're not leaving me? Not leaving us?"

"I love you, I want you as long as you let me in your lives. I just think it would be best for me to move out. We started this so fast, I think I need my own space to make sure this relationship has it's best shot," I explain. I need to maintain some independence if I don't want to get lost in *us*. This has to be the way to do that. I just hope Lucy will understand that.

She doesn't answer, but her lips crush mine. In a desperate moment of finding closeness, I need this too. I kiss her back, but stop when I lock the door. She crawls into my bed, already undressed, her clothes strewn about my floor. I do the same, as she watches me, as if trying to lock this moment into a memory.

Our lips meet again, desperate for each other. Hands melting into each other's bodies as we try to savor every second of this moment. It feels like a goodbye despite this not being over. This is the end of something and we both know it. So she kisses my neck lightly, nibbling my earlobe and blowing in my ear. If this is going to be our last time in this bed, we are going to make the most of it.

I climb on top, reaching for my nightstand and pulling out my strap on. "I want to make love to you," I whisper to her lips. She nods, with a look of worry crosses her face. I quickly kiss her forehead, brushing away any fears she might have.

"I'm not going anywhere," I remind her.

She nods but doesn't speak, her hands all over my chest and hips as she pulls me in closer to her. I pull away just long enough to put it on and position myself between her legs. Brushing her blonde curls out of her face, I look into her bright blue eyes. She wraps her legs around my waist and I lean down to kiss her, her lips enveloping mine. Her hands touch my waist, trailing down to my ass and she grabs me with a light squeeze, pulling me even closer to her. If we could be any closer, we'd be one.

"I love you," I whisper, my hand caressing her cheek. She closes her eyes and leans into my hand, smiling.

"I love you too," she whispers back. I've never been this close to someone, romantically or sexually, and I'd be lying if I said it didn't scare the hell out of me. But it also feels right. Being with Lucy in this way just feels natural, which is how I know I don't want to lose her.

She reaches a hand between us and guides me inside her. She's soaked, I can feel her against my thighs dripping from her core. I begin moving my hips slowly, looking into her eyes as I hold the headboard to keep my pace. I know I am teasing her but for once she isn't begging for more, she is enjoying every second of it. I move my hips, pumping them into hers, her breath becoming shallow with each movement.

"Kiss me," she moans and I bend down to kiss her. She's needy, her hands wrapping around my neck just as her legs are around my waist. I give myself to her, in every way I can. Pressing my lips to hers, letting our bodies connect and falling asleep next to each other. We don't say another word tonight, too afraid of what might come out.

In the morning, I email my school that I'm taking the TA job. It feels right as I fill out all the forms and send them back. It also helps knowing I'll be able to pay for college without touching the money Lucy gave me for nannying Noel. Something about using it just doesn't seem right to me anymore. Not when it didn't feel like a job.

Noel knows my last day is right before the new year. We thought it be best not to prolong the inevitable, especially when Lucy is off from work anyway. He is upset when we tell him, but with the promise of me visiting and hanging out with him, he understands. I think a little better than Lucy does.

"You can still hang out with me, right?" he asks.

"Of course." I pause to look at Lucy.

"Nanny Morgan and I are dating, so she might be coming over to see me too," Lucy adds.

"That's cool," Noel says with a shrug. I can tell Lucy was worried about officially telling him but that's the thing about raising kids right, if you don't make it a big deal, they won't freak out.

We spend the last few days together in the house. Noel, Lucy, and I watch movies, play his video games, and drink way too much hot cocoa together. Every night Lucy sneaks into my bed when Noel's asleep, and we just cuddle or read together. It feels like we're waiting for a storm to pass, but to me, it feels more like the beginning of something rather than the end.

I started looking for an apartment in the city, something not too far from campus and not too far from Lucy. Bella and Ellie offered to let me stay in their apartments but I think it's time I live on my own, especially now that I can afford it. The TA job will take up most of my days, but I only need four classes to graduate. Four easy classes that I saved for my last semester to make my life easier. Thank you, past me. It is like things are finally starting to fall into place for me.

TWENTY-SEVEN

Lucy

I watch as Lucy and her friends take all the boxes out of the apartment. It feels wrong but I couldn't help her. Noel's at his dad's so he doesn't have to be a witness to this. I don't know if I could handle his feelings on top of my own today.

"I think that's everything," Morgan says with a sigh. She hadn't brought a lot with her, I guess she didn't own too much.

"Okay." I nod.

"Luce, I love you."

"I love you too." I pause. "Are you sure about this?" I ask again. I know it seems desperate but I need to know that she's sure about this.

"I am. I think it's the best way for us to be together." She kisses my lips lightly and I close the door behind her. For the first time in months, the guest room is empty as it is no longer Morgan's room.

I walk to close her door when I spot a book on her nightstand. Of course Morgan would leave a book behind. I pick it up and a note falls to the floor.

Dear Luce,

I know you think this means the end of us, but to me this is only the beginning. I was never someone looking for a relationship or a forever with someone. I liked being alone, I was good at it. But that night I met you in the bar, you changed everything for me. I never could've imagined this is how things would turn out for us, but I want you to know I'm happy. For the first time in my life I'm not alone. I know moving out might have felt like me leaving, but I really think this is the best way for me to keep some independence while we grow as a couple together. I want to spend the rest of my Christmases with you and Noel, fuck it. The rest of my life with the two of you. So I hope this little space brings us closer together as I finish my degree and then I can come home to you. Because even though it might feel like me leaving, I plan to spend every free moment drinking hot cocoa with you, or kissing you, or playing video games I don't understand with Noel. It'll be like I never left. Meanwhile, you and I can figure out if this thing is meant to be a forever, like I hope it can be.

Love,

Morgan

P.S. I left you this book because you looked like you could use a laugh.'

I fold the note and look at the book, *44 Chapters About 4 Men* by **BB Easton**. I'm already laughing at the title, *she wanted me to read a book about men?* I hold the book close to my chest and close my eyes. As much as I hate Morgan leaving, I know it is what is best for her. What will hopefully be best for us.

Noel and I usually spend New Year's Eve at my apartment, drinking fake champagne and eating little finger foods. But this year we decided to surprise Morgan at her new apartment, because there's no one else we'd rather spend the new year with.

"What are you guys doing here?!" She opens the door with a huge smile on her face.

"Should we have called?" A worry runs through me as I realize maybe she had other plans for tonight.

"You never have to call." She presses her lips to mine and invites us inside.

It's smaller than I expect, the living room and kitchen being combined in one room, with her bedroom door visible down a short hallway. It's only half decorated, boxes still strewn about the place, but there's a couch and a tv for us to watch the ball drop.

"I thought we could ring in the new year together," I suggest.

"I would love that." She smiles. "I'm sorry about the mess, I'm still in the process of unpacking."

"Don't worry about it." I take a seat on the couch and Noel plops down next to me.

"What do you guys usually do for the new year?" she asks as she reaches for the remote.

"We watch the ball drop," Noel answers.

"What if we just watched some movies until then?"

"Sounds good, as long as it's not a romance," Morgan makes a face and Noel nods.

"Yeah, nothing with gross kissing."

"Excuse me, I actually like romance movies!" I fake gasp.

"We know," Morgan and Noel say in unison.

We watch some action hero movie and order a pizza. Noel ends up playing his switch on the floor and Morgan and I cuddle on the couch. Eventually, we switch to watching those cheesy New Year's Eve specials where they countdown around the world. Noel's passed out on the couch and Morgan and I break open a bottle of real Champagne to cheers to the new year.

10...

"Wait! We should make a wish for the new year," I say with a smile.

7...

"A wish? I've never heard of that."

5...

"Like a manifestation. Something you want to happen next year," I say quickly.

3...

180

"I have everything I could possibly wish for right here," Morgan says with a shy smile.

1!

She presses her lips to mine and we both take a sip of our champagne. For the first time in my life, I didn't have anything to wish for either. My son is happy and healthy and I've finally met the love of my life, and I am lucky enough that she loves me back.

Epilogue

MORGAN

"Are you sure you're okay?" Lucy worries holding my hand tightly.

"I'm sure, it's just some stairs I'll be fine." I shake my head and she sighs. It's been eight months of this, you think I'd be used to it by now.

"I'm sorry, I just want to make sure my wife and daughter are doing okay." Lucy pats my ugly sweater covered belly. I wasn't the one who decided to go to an ugly sweater Christmas party when I was almost nine months pregnant. But it was Ellie's party and even though I could say no to my best friend, apparently my wife couldn't.

"Mom, they're fine. Morgan literally went ice skating last week. She's chill." Noel says looking up from his cell phone. I swear that thing was attached to him more than his old switch used to be.

"Excuse me?" Lucy's eyes go wide and Noel and I share a look.

"Uhh," we both say in unison. Ice skating was supposed to be our little secret.

"That's what I thought. You really are trying to give me a heart attack in my old age." Lucy sighs. She was barely 45 but she loved to remind me how 'old' she was. Especially when I was doing something to worry her.

"Hey, I'm sorry. But we're okay and I can handle some stairs, let's just get to this party because I am starving." I smile. Pressing my lips to hers, she relaxes a bit.

"Gross." Noel makes a face as he rings the doorbell.

"Noel! You're getting huge!" Ellie answers the door, clearly already dipping into the holiday eggnog.

"If you say the same thing to me, I'll punch you." I warn Ellie who laughs.

"No, that's my Godchild in there. It's good she's growing so nicely." She pats my swollen belly and smiles.

"Excuse me, I think that's my Godchild." Bella steps in.

"Why don't you invite us in and then you can argue over who's Godchild it is?" Lucy says with a laugh.

"Oh yes! Come on in!" Ellie makes way and we all take off our coats. Well, except me. I was like ten thousand degrees thanks to being a human incubator so I did not wear a winter coat these days.

"There's food in the living room and drinks in the kitchen," Ellie smiles.

"Let me take your coats," Bella grabs them and heads down the hallway toward Ellie's room.

"I can introduce you, but I think you know everyone. Noel, some of my friends brought their kids and they're upstairs playing on the xbox." Ellie explains, he takes one look at us, we nod and he's up the stairs like lightning.

"You have an Xbox?" I look at Ellie raising an eyebrow.

"Uh no, that would be Reese's who I'm pretty sure is up there playing with them." She says rolling her eyes.

"Let's find you some food," Lucy takes my hand as Ellie joins the party.

"How do you know I'm hungry?" I raise an eyebrow.

"Is that a trick question?" Lucy says with a laugh.

"Fine, but it's your daughter who's always hungry." I groan as we make our way to the food. There was a buffet style of tons of pastas and Italian food across what was their dining room table.

"My daughter," Lucy smiles. She likes that whenever the baby is kicking or doing something I don't like she suddenly becomes *her* daughter. On a good day, she's both of our daughters.

Despite using Lucy's egg and my body as a human incubator, she was both of our daughter. It was an easy decision, I wanted Noel to have a biological sibling and have the chance to carry Lucy's baby. It was safer for me to carry the baby due to my age, and it gave me the chance to be pregnant, not that I was likely to do it again. Being pregnant isn't a walk in the park, I had three weeks until my due date and I was praying everyday she'd come sooner. At least now that we were out of the woods. I had spent the first few months of my first teaching job, pregnant as hell. Now that I was finally on winter break and maternity leave, I could afford to have this baby.

"Your daughter wants a big plate with lots of everything." I point out and take a seat in one of the chairs. I was like a walking blimp these days and I got exhausted easily.

Suddenly there's a commotion coming from the living room. A blonde and brunette woman are being dared to kiss under the mistletoe. It takes them a second but then one of them goes for it and the rest is history. I cheer along with the crowd and Lucy shakes her head.

"What? I love a good mistletoe kiss." I smirk.

"You referring to one of our first kisses?" She smiles.

"Or maybe our wedding." A Christmas wedding seemed only fitting for us. Complete with mistletoe hanging above us for our first kiss.

"I love you," She says bending over to kiss me.

"I love you too," I whisper against her lips. She leans in again, this time gently tugging on my bottom lip with her teeth. *Was she trying to turn me on?*

"I want you," Lucy whispers.

"Right now?" I try to hide my surprise.

"Right now." She nods.

I shouldn't be surprised, Lucy and I had always had an active sex life. But I worried when I got pregnant that might take a hiatus, when in reality it seemed to have the opposite effect. Lately she couldn't keep her hands off me, not that I was complaining. She could make me feel like the most beautiful woman in the room despite how I looked or felt otherwise.

"Where?"

"Trust me," She takes my hand and I stand, following her into the kitchen. She looks around to see if anyone is nearby and then smiles mischievously at me.

"Climb up," she pats the counter like it's no big deal and I drop my jaw.

"Are you serious?" I knew I was adventurous but there were people only two rooms away. We could get caught at any second.

"I'm serious, I want to eat you out." She whispers against my ear and I'm soaked.

Backing up, I try to maneuver onto the counter, she holds one hip and I hop up in one motion easier than expected. She touches my thighs lightly, spreading them open just enough to open them and slide down my panties. She sticks them in her purse and comes back to me. I keep my eye on the open doorway, wondering if we'd hear anyone before we see them. With the loud music playing in the other room, it was unlikely. But before I could protest, Lucy was diving between my thighs.

"Oh!" I throw my head back in pleasure, forgetting where we are for a moment. Lucy stops, ducking out form under my skirt and gives me a look. I nod, reminding myself to be quiet and she continues. Her head under my skirt, thankfully I chose to wear a longer one tonight.

Lucy's fingers slide inside me gently. First one and then a second, with her tongue dancing across my clit in easy circles. My clit was on fire as she touched me, all my nerves seemingly greater now. I grip the edge of the counter, knowing it wouldn't take long for me to cum. Lucy reaches up to paw at my gigantic breasts and my nipples harden instantly through the thin bralette.

"I'm so close," I whisper, not knowing or caring if Lucy can hear me. But she must because she continues just a little bit faster, her tongue lapping up my juices. I'm on the verge of wanting to scream her name when I hear someone coming. I'm about to say something to Lucy but at the same time, I start to orgasm and I can't stop.

"Oh my gosh!" Ellie's voice is nothing but background noise as I throw my head back in pleasure, closing my eyes with Lucy's lips on mine. She ducks out from under my skirt, her face red as she wipes her mouth off with the back of her arm.

"Fuck," I hop off the counter and lean into Lucy, hiding of embarrassment from my best friend seeing me orgasm.

"Is it safe?" She calls holding a hand over her eyes.

"It's safe." Lucy says with a laugh.

"I'm so sorry—" Ellie cuts me off.

"We will never speak of it again, I'm glad you're still getting some in your billionth month of pregnancy. I hope if I ever get pregnant, Reese will want me that much too." Ellie says with a wink. "Now, I just needed a drink and to clean the counter where your ass has been."

"I'm sorry," Lucy starts but Ellie stops her.

"Never. Speak. Of. It. Again."

We nod and make our way back to the party. Lucy holding my hand, she pulls me in for an elongated kiss. I lean in, post orgasm happy but also happy to be in her arms.

"Why don't we get you some food," Lucy suggests.

"Sure," I pause. "As long as you go wash those hands first." I tease.

Lucy laughs and makes her way back to the kitchen where Ellie and her turn bright shades of red. She comes back to get me some food and we check on Noel. Well, Lucy checks on Noel because I was not managing anymore stairs tonight. So I find myself a spot on the couch and make sure I'm not flashing anyone since Lucy hadn't given back my panties. Something I was pretty sure she did on purpose. She joins me on the couch, holding my hand and we get to know new people, and I'm relieved we made it. If this was how my life went for the rest of time, I would be happy. The baby kicks, as if to agree and I smile as Lucy's hand joins mine on our growing family.

Also by Shannon O'Connor

Electric Love

Butterflies in Paris

All's Fair in Love & Vegas

I Saw Mommy Kissing the Nanny

Lucky to Be Yours

Ugly Sweater Christmas

ANTHOLOGIES

A Taste Of You

An Appetite for You

Personal Foul

POETRY

For Always

Holding on to Nothing

Say it Everyday

Midnights in a Mustang

Five More Minutes

When Lust Was Enough

Isolation

All of Me

Lost Moments

Cosmic

Acknowledgments

A huge thank you to M Leigh Morhaime for always Beta reading for me and encouraging me not to give up even on the hardest of days.

To my ARC and street team who encourage me to keep writing and help me in so many ways. You guys mean the world to me.

To my Teddy bear, I love you more than life. Thank you for always being my little publicist and telling anyone who's holding a book that "mama writes books". Your joy keeps me going, I hope I make you proud.

To my family who watches my little bear when inspiration strikes, who supports my career and offers advice along the way, I love you all.

To my grandma, who convinced me to write a Christmas book this year. Please don't read it.

About the Author

Shannon O'Connor is a twenty-something, bisexual, self-published poet of several books and counting. She released her first novel, *Electric Love* in 2021 and is currently working on several sapphic romance novels. She believes there is a lack of positive Female/Female romances in the world, and wants to make them more accessible. She is often found in coffee shops, probably writing about someone she shouldn't be.

Heat. Heart. & A Bit of Both.

Check out more work & updates on:

Facebook Group: https://www.facebook.com/groups/shanssquad

Website: https://shanoconnor.com

Lightning Source UK Ltd.
Milton Keynes UK
UKHW021809181222
414118UK00009B/68